8

C000066697

DO YOU
LOVE YOUR
M♡M
and Her Two-Hit
Multi-Target
Attacks
?

Dachima Inaka

Illustration by **Iida Pochi.**

MEDHI

A high school Cleric. This time she's less about the evil within and more focused on fighting in the name of friendship.

"There's no saving her now..."

MASATO OOSUKI

A Normal Hero. He leaves Mamako to handle the threat to the world and goes all out trying to get Porta back.

"Calm down a minute!"

"Fight? You can't mean that!"

WISE

Her magic may always get sealed, but this high school Sage remains undaunted.

"If I win, I'll be able to protect my mommy!"

PORTA

A Traveling Merchant who is actually the final member of the Four Heavenly Kings of the Libere Rebellion.

SHIRASE

A mother serving as the producer for the all-mom idol unit MOM-3.

"You got a problem with me? Spit it out! Family squabbles are my thing! I'm Mom Idol Number Two!"

KAZUNO

Wise's mother. Doesn't hate the idol thing as much as she claims. Definitely the type who's along for the ride.

"Now there's a beautiful smile! Love the enthusiasm."

"My love is boundless! I love you sooo much! Let me give you a biiig hug! I'm Mom Idol Number One!"

"Being strict is an expression of love! Together we'll strive for greater heights! I'm Mom Idol Number Three!"

MAMAKO OOSUKI

The kind of mom who's the life of the party. Has zero qualms about becoming an idol to save the world.

MEDHIMAMA

Medhi's mother. Resistant to becoming an idol, but once she signs on, she's surprisingly committed.

Mama☆Mama☆Magic (MMMMMAGIC)

Lyrics: Dachima Inaka

(Mammaaa Maaamaaama Maaamaaa)

(Mammaaa Maaamaaama Maaagic!)

(Mamako) When I greet you with "Good morning!"

(Mamako) You scowl and turn your back

I know you're just embarrassed

But if I say that, you might get mad again

(Kazuno) You're always mouthing off

(Memama) Guess you need more discipline

(Mamako) Some special mommy magic

To make you turn and face us in a snap

(Mamamama Maaagic!)

Only one in all this world

(Kazuno) A bond that can't be broken

(Memama) Always at your side

(Mamako) Squeezing you oh so tight

(Mamamama Maaagic!)

The miracle of your birth

Greater than the Earth

Deeper than the ocean

A love that knows no bounds

(Mammaaa Maaamaaama Maaagic!)

CONTENTS

Dachima Inaka

VOLUME 8

DACHIMA INAKA

Illustration by IIDA POCHI.

YEN
ON

New York

Do You Love Your Mom and Her Two-Hit Multi-Target Attacks?, Vol. 8

▶ Dachima Inaka

▶ Translation by Andrew Cunningham

▶ Cover art by Iida Pochi.

This book is a work of fiction. Names, characters, places, and incidents are the product of the author's imagination or are used fictitiously. Any resemblance to actual events, locales, or persons, living or dead, is coincidental.

First Yen On Edition: February 2021

Yen On is an imprint of Yen Press, LLC.
The Yen On name and logo are trademarks of Yen Press, LLC.

The publisher is not responsible for websites (or their content) that are not owned by the publisher.

▶ Yen On
150 West 30th Street, 19th Floor
New York, NY 10001

▶ Visit us at yenpress.com
facebook.com/yenpress
twitter.com/yenpress
yenpress.tumblr.com
instagram.com/yenpress

Library of Congress Cataloging-in-Publication Data
Names: Inaka, Dachima, author. | Pochi., Iida, illustrator. | Cunningham, Andrew, 1979– translator.
Title: Do you love your mom and her two-target attacks? / Dachima Inaka ; illustration by Iida Pochi. ; translation by Andrew Cunningham.
Other titles: Tsujo kogeki ga zentai kogeki de 2kai kogeki no okasan wa suki desuka?. English
Description: First Yen On edition. | New York : Yen On, 2018–
Identifiers: LCCN 2018030739 | ISBN 9781975328009 (v. 1 : pbk.) | ISBN 9781975328375 (v. 2 : pbk.) | ISBN 9781975328399 (v. 3 : pbk.) | ISBN 9781975328412 (v. 4 : pbk.) | ISBN 9781975359423 (v. 5 : pbk.) | ISBN 9781975359430 (v. 6 : pbk.) | ISBN 9781975306311 (v. 7 : pbk.) | ISBN 9781975306328 (v. 8 : pbk.)
Subjects: LCSH: Virtual reality—Fiction.
Classification: LCC PL871.5.N35 T7813 2018 | DDC 895.63/6—dc23
LC record available at https://lccn.loc.gov/2018030739

ISBNs: 978-1-9753-0632-8 (paperback)
       978-1-9753-0952-7 (ebook)

10 9 8 7 6 5 4 3 2 1

LSC-C

Printed in the United States of America

Prologue   The Producer Vanishes

The real world. Japan. Tokyo. Chiyoda Ward. Nagata District.

It was a rainy day. The buildings seemed huddled together, their sodden heads drooping. A gloomy sight.

"If only it were sunny…," Shirase muttered, brushing the drops of water off her suit. "This just makes a grim task all the more grim."

Shirase was visiting a particular office building along with several male personnel.

"Welcome. How can I help—?"

"We don't have an appointment, but our business is compulsory, so we'll be going straight in."

"Uh…r-right! Please proceed."

One glimpse of the permit their higher-ups had provided, and the receptionist waved them onward to their destination.

"We'll take up positions in the hallways in the event our target tries to flee. You proceed as planned, Shirase."

"I am to consider my own safety my first priority and take no unnecessary risks, correct?"

"Exactly. If the target chooses to ignore warnings and resist, call for help, and we'll handle things from there. It's your call to make."

The male personnel fanned out to their positions.

On her own, Shirase headed toward the office labeled PLANNING AND DEVELOPMENT SECTION #4.

"I feel very strongly this is *not* my job…but I was charged with the task of informing her. As my name is Shirase, I can hardly refuse."

Shirase entered the room, ignoring staff surprised by the sudden intrusion. She moved swiftly through the rows of desks to the boss's office at the back.

She paused for a moment outside the door to pull an envelope from her briefcase.

The envelope contained a document. A formal salutation followed by a pile of legalese that boiled down to, "We're cutting off negotiations and resorting to force." A declaration of management's verdict.

Their final notice.

"I had intended to leave this to the heroic family once again…but the executives moved faster than anticipated," Shirase said, speaking a bit too loud for someone talking to herself. "Considering the target's credentials, perhaps they had no choice, but personally, I consider it a shame."

She waited a *very* long time before opening the office door.

"Pardon me. We last spoke during the Materland incident. Once again, my name is Shirase, and I'm here to inform you… Oh?"

The office was extremely tidy, no personal possessions at all. Just a desk and a shredder.

On the desk were a ballpoint pen, a few document pages, and a desktop computer, the monitor covered in Post-it notes.

There was no sign of the target.

"She wasn't here…? No, that seems unlikely."

Shirase pressed her finger to the document on the desk and found the ink not yet dry. Someone had clearly been working here moments before she had arrived.

Then Shirase saw the computer screen. The browser was open to a familiar address:

www8.cao.go.jp/ksn/mmmmmorpg…

The same address Shirase had typed to send a certain boy into the game world.

The target's location was clear.

"Our journey here may have been in vain, but I welcome this outcome."

One drawer of the desk was open a crack. Inside was a knitting kit and a photograph, the frame of it covered in adorable decorations.

Shirase picked up the frame, gazing at the photograph and nodding to herself.

"A chance still remains…so I must hasten to play my part."

She put the office's sole personal touch, a precious treasure the owner could not bear to be without, back in the drawer.

And then she *accidentally* dropped the final notice in the shredder on her way out.

*　　*　　*

On that day, an uninvited guest entered the world of *MMMMMORPG* (working title).

This was a disaster. That someone would wreak havoc on the entire world.

They appeared at the edge of the game world in a howling blizzard, their eyes filled with loathing for everything that world represented.

They fixed their gaze on something occurring far, far off in the distance.

Not a soul noticed that gaze…save for one single person.

Chapter 1 Things That I Believed Were Forever: Parents, Money, and...Porta?

It happened suddenly.

The hero's party were exploring a grassy field, when...

"Huh? ...Mm?"

...the Traveling Merchant, Porta, stopped in her tracks, staring at the sky to the north.

Nothing but a small cloud drifted slowly along, yet her eyes stayed fixed to it.

She remained like that for over a minute.

Long enough that her friends began to get worried.

"Um...what's gotten into Porta?" Masato asked.

"Beats me...," Wise replied.

"Doesn't seem like she's spotted any monsters...," Medhi said.

All three were at a loss.

"Oh?" Mamako, the hero's mother, said. It seemed she'd sensed something. "Hmm...yes...there is, well..."

"Uh, Mom, what's going on? Clue us in."

"Hmm...I'm not quite sure how to put this... It's just a nebulous anxious feeling."

"Can you be more specific...?"

"I wish I could, but it's definitely upsetting. Like I have to do *this* to calm myself."

Mamako wrapped her arms around Masato's head, pulling him in tight against her chest. "Oh, that's much better." "Leggo!" Stroking the head of her beloved son was *such* a relief!

But it was definitely a destabilizing influence on his psyche, so he soon wriggled out from her embrace.

"Anyway, if you're sensing it, Mom, then there's definitely something going on..."

"Yeah...," Wise agreed. "Oh, maybe it's, like, a hidden threat to the world that's emerged?"

"You think she's sensing the appearance of a demon lord?" wondered Medhi.

"Wait, wait. If that's true, then as the Hero, this is my field. Let me take a look."

Masato stared at the sky to the north, focusing his mind.

Ten seconds passed. Thirty.

"Well? Go on, fess up. The sooner you apologize, the better."

"Honesty will prove your salvation. We promise to send you off with warm smiles."

"Argh...!"

Clearly neither girl expected anything from him. How demoralizing.

But that only further motivated him to pick up something! ...That said, this was looking more and more pointless by the minute—

No, wait.

...Mm? Is that...?

It could be a trick of the light, or an eye floater.

But he could see a very thin thread that appeared ready to snap at any moment. Just looking at it made him anxious.

And it seemed to be reaching toward Porta...

"Sorry!" Porta said suddenly. "I was kinda out of it for a moment there!"

"Er...?" Masato's concentration instantly dissipated. "W-well, uh, welcome back."

Porta came running to him, and he looked her over carefully, but saw no signs of anything stringlike. Maybe he'd been seeing things...

"Masato? Is there something on me?"

"Er, no...I dunno how to put this... It was like I saw a sort of nebulous anxiety..."

"How can you see anxiety?!"

"Masato, don't strain yourself. We know better."

"That doesn't sound like a compliment...but fair enough; I'm pretty confused about it myself."

"So what were you looking at, Porta?" asked Mamako.

"I don't know!" Porta replied. "I felt like my eyes were drawn to something, but I don't know what!"

She wasn't the type to lie.

"Right...we felt like we sensed something, but nobody's clear what.

It's alarming, but…worrying about it isn't gonna get us anywhere. So I guess we should just drop it?" Masato looked around the group. "Well, then, let's do what we came for! Today's goal is to try out the new combat style I thought up!"

It was an indisputable fact that Mamako dominated all combat. The instant an encounter began, she would sweep the field clear of enemies.

The time for mutiny was nigh.

"We, the children, have nonetheless grown stronger by the day! Come, comrades! Let us demonstrate our power!"

"Sure, sure, we'll pretend to go along with it for now."

"The results are a foregone conclusion, but for the time being, we'll grin and bear it."

"Ladies, a little enthusiasm, if you could?"

"Um, Ma-kun, Mommy hasn't heard any explanation for this new combat style…"

"Mom, you just attack at will, like you always have. Our goal here is to see how we can fit in around your attacks."

"Okay, then. Mommy will just do her thing!"

"Great. Now, to make this new combat style work, one member of our party's actions will be extra critical. Namely…"

The party's item master and mental care expert. The twelve-year-old Traveling Merchant named…

"Porta! We're counting on you!"

"Right! I'll do my best!"

The sincerity in her eyes gave them courage. Also, it was really cute. "Adorbs!" "Eep!" Masato's fingers danced around her cheeks.

It was time to begin.

As always, the party set off across the field. Just walking around in circles…

"Oh—whoops!" Porta found some monsters, but quickly clapped her hands over her mouth.

Before announcing the enemies' arrival, she quickly ran over to Mamako's side.

"Oh my, what is it?"

"Mama! Come here!"

Porta took a picnic blanket out of her shoulder bag and spread it out on the ground.

Then she took out a tea set, and some sweets, and laid them out over top.

By the time combat began, the tea party was under way!

"Oh, that looks lovely. I suppose it's time for a break!"

"Yes! Mama, you have tea with me, while…!"

The moment Mamako sat down, Porta shot the others a look. *To the left*, it said.

They nodded and ran in the direction she'd indicated.

"Right! All according to plan! Let us put our knowledge and hard work to the test! We'll find these monsters before Mom does and… There they are!"

They located the monster horde: a bunch of wolf- and spider-type monsters on the ground…

…and several huge bird monsters in the sky.

"Hell yes, flying enemies! Leave them to me! Here goes!"

Masato went first. Savoring the delight of getting an attack off before Mamako, he swung the Holy Sword of the Heavens as hard as he could.

"Enemies that fly are no match for…me!"

A beam of light shot toward the screeching bird monsters.

There were several of them, and only one beam…but the beam split, changing into four hawks, each tracking a different target.

"Yes, there it is! I'm growing stronger! Go!"

"Heh…even Masato has his moments. Right, then land enemies are up to the ultimate Sage, yours truly!"

"*…Spara la magia per mirare… Morte!*"

"Wha—Medhi! Leave some for me! *…Spara la magia per mirare… Fiamma Cerchio!* And! *Fiamma Cerchio!*"

Medhi's instant death spell went off while Wise was talking, but Wise quickly rushed through her chant, and chain cast two spells.

Large magic circles appeared above and below the land monsters, spouting columns of flames.

Meanwhile, a reaper sped between the fires, slashing monsters and removing their souls.

"Nicely done, Wise, Medhi! Man, this is great! This new combat style is a massive success!"

"Even if it just amounts to Porta distracting Mamako," noted Wise.

"I can't help but feel we could just ask her nicely to let us go first…," said Medhi.

"Oh...," said Masato. "I mean, that's true, but...isn't that kinda... depressing?"

"This way she'll be forced to entertain Mamako during every battle."

"And the amount of extra sugar and water Mamako will consume during those tea parties would really add up."

"Uh...well, we can cross that bridge when we come to it! For now, let's enjoy this battle! It's still our turn! Bwa-ha-ha-ha!"

Even Masato knew this combat style was probably already canceled, but for the moment he was still fighting.

Mamako was watching with a smile.

"They've all gotten so good at fighting!"

"Yes! Masato, Wise, and Medhi are all very strong!"

"And Porta, you've gotten so good at supporting everyone! You even prepared this lovely party. I was so surprised!"

"I'm glad to be able to do so many things now!"

"Hee-hee. Well, it makes me so happy to see how everyone's grown. But..."

Mamako's smile dimmed.

"But I do feel a little left out."

"Huh? Left out?"

"Yes. Children grow up, and you can let them do so many things, and soon Mommy doesn't have anything to do, and...I start to wonder if they really need a mommy."

"That's not true! I want a mommy!"

A sudden shriek.

Mamako, the three children fighting, the monsters, even the instant death reaper—everyone froze, startled.

Porta looked ready to burst into tears, but then she gasped, and recovered.

"Um...s-sorry, that was really loud! I just, uh..."

"It's okay, Porta, dear. I'm sorry I said something so upsetting."

"N-no! It's not your fault, Mama. But I...I just thought not needing a mommy is wrong, so..."

"I see."

Porta hung her head, and Mamako reached out and rubbed it gently.

"So you still need a mommy, Porta. That's lovely to hear. In that case, let me go show everyone they still need Mommy around."

"O-okay! Please do!"

Mamako slowly stood up, a Holy Sword in each hand.

Then—"Hyah!"—Mamako attacked. Rock spikes shot up, water bullets fired, and the rest of the monsters were instantly slain. "Wha—heeyyyyyyyyy!" Masato yelled, but the battle was over.

"This is Mommy's power! See?"

"Yes! Mommies are amazing! We need mommies!"

"That's right. You still need Mommy. I'll stay right here with you. Hee-hee-hee."

She shot Porta an impish wink.

Then Mamako turned and went over to Masato. "Mom!" "Oh? What?" Her son looked ready to protest. Another family squabble?

Porta watched them closely.

"I do want a mommy…my mommy…," she whispered.

She turned and looked north again.

With their new combat style experiment concluded, the party returned to the nearby town.

"Well, we knew it was doomed to fail when Masato thought of it."

"And what a failure it was. I feel like the specific cause was an excess of faith in his own growth."

"No, no, we can't be sure of that!" Masato protested. "It might still work! This isn't a style that can work during regular combat, but it might still be really effective at key moments! So…"

Not wanting to waste a moment, they went straight to the Adventurers Guild.

Directly to the board where quests were posted.

"To test the full potential, we need a quest!"

"Why a quest?"

"The reason is simple. I believe the style I invented may work wonders in boss battles. I know it will! So we need a hunt quest to test it on."

"I feel like even if we try this, Mamako will just sit there enjoying her tea and cakes while defeating the boss with her free hand…," said Medhi.

"Don't even suggest that! You'll jinx us for sure! A-anyway, that's the plan, so help me find a suitable quest!"

"Got it! I'll do my best!"

"Mommy will, too! I'll show you how reliable I am!"

"That's...also frustrating but...go ahead."

Wise, Medhi, Masato, Mamako, and Porta lined up along the giant bulletin board, checking the postings one by one.

Some postings were just text, while others had photorealistic illustrations. And the board was packed full of them, in all shapes and sizes—over a hundred in all. It could be a real challenge locating the exact type you wanted.

"A specific enemy, one we can quickly get to and defeat...hmm..."

You'd think a hunt quest or two would be lying around, but of course, when you really wanted one, there was nothing. It was all material gathering or fetch quests.

Masato moved down the row, and his shoulder bumped Mamako's.

"Whoops, sorry."

"Oh, don't worry, Ma-kun. You can stay as close to me as you like!"

"No, thanks."

Masato pulled away, but Mamako clung to him. "...Yo." "Hee-hee-hee." It was like iron filings being dragged by a magnet.

Obnoxious...but maybe it worked in his favor.

He actually had something he'd been wanting to ask her.

"...Uh, Mom, question for you. Why did Porta suddenly start yelling while we were fighting? What was that about?"

"Oh, that..."

"Whoa?!"

Before Mamako could answer, Porta let out a yelp of surprise.

Masato was worried she'd heard them whispering, but apparently not.

She had a quest posting in her hand and was gaping at it, frozen stiff.

"Wh-what's up, Porta? You found an astonishingly good quest?"

"Whaaa...oh, um... N-no, I didn't!"

"You didn't? Then what's that in your hand?" asked Mamako.

"Eeek...i-it's nothing!"

She crumpled up the page and hid it behind her, shaking her head as hard as she could.

This was waaaay beyond suspicious.

"Uh, Porta?" *Grin.*

"Porta, dear?" *Grin.*

"It's nothing!" Porta squeaked, rummaging around behind her back. Then she held up both hands "See?!"

Ah-ha. Nothing in her hands... Yeah, no.

"Okay, Porta. Turn to the right!"

"Um, um...I-I don't know right from left so I can't turn!"

"Right is the hand you hold your chopsticks in! You hold the bowl in your left," said Mamako.

"Tell you what, I'll go around Porta's right side, and Mom, you take the left. I wonder what Porta's hiiiiding..."

"Eeeeek?! I'm not hiding anythiiiiing!"

Masato and Mamako gradually surrounded the panicked Porta when...

"Oh, Masato. Do you have a spare moment?"

...Medhi suddenly stepped up behind him.

"Sorry, Medhi, we're busy investigating Porta. Can it wait? ...All right, Porta! Behave. We don't want to have to hurt you! Heh-heh-heh."

"You can listen to me or get arrested for being a creep. Which do you prefer?"

"I always have time for you, Medhi."

Realizing his last statement *had* been pretty creepy, Masato elected to obey.

Medhi showed him a quest. It was written on high-quality paper, with gold foil—clearly a top-class quest.

Investigate the earth and the ocean, it read.

The quest giver was the Queen of Catharn (who was actually Catharn's queen).

"A request from the queen...to investigate the earth and ocean... the investigation range is the entire world, including worlds in other servers, so also Materland... That's...quite a scale."

"That means something's happening that needs investigating. I'm a little concerned."

"Yeah. Plus, we know the queen, and she and Mom got pretty chummy...so we should probably go along with it."

"Yes, Mommy agrees."

"I do, too! That quest is the most important thing right now!" Porta agreed, very enthusiastically.

Maybe a bit too enthusiastically. "Mm? Porta?" "Porta, dear?" "Eeek!" She was very obviously trying to turn their attention to the queen's quest.

But before Masato could go after her again, someone smacked the back of his head.

"Yo, creep. C'mere. I found a concerning quest, too."

"I absolutely refute the creep designation, just so you know. But what is it, Wise?"

Wise showed him a posting rolled up into a cylinder—all of ordinary quality.

It read: *Provide information about unnaturally rapid growth in children.*

And the request came from Mone of the Mom Shop.

"Mone's looking for information? Unnaturally rapid growth in children…what's going on?"

"I dunno, but that's what it says. Can't very well ignore that, either, can we?"

"Right. If something's happening to children, that could be bad."

"Yes! I agree! That quest is our top priority!"

Porta was being obvious again. "Mm? Porta?" "Eeek!" Masato wanted nothing more than to hound her for answers and torment her…

But this was no laughing matter.

"Guess we'd better cancel our plans and take care of these."

"Wow, how noble of you, Masato! I was expecting a brattier response."

"You think that little of me?! …Still, how do we handle this?"

An investigation of the ocean and the earth. Sudden growth in children. And mounting concerns about Porta's behavior.

He looked over the two postings and stole another glance at Porta's highly suspicious fidgeting.

It was time for the Hero Masato to make a deci—

"I'm just so worried about the children! Let's go to the Mom Shop first and hear Mone out. Right, Ma-kun?"

"Yep. I knew it. Go right ahead, then."

"Okay! My transport spell will take us there in a snap!" said Wise.

Mamako's decision set the party in motion.

"So there we have it… You must be so glad, aren't you, Porta?" asked Mamako.

"Y-yes! I'm very reliev—I mean, n-no! I'm not hiding anything!"

They raced out of the Adventurers Guild. The party was surrounded by the light of the transport spell and swept away from the town.

Masato and his group landed at the entrance to the Catharn capital.

Passersby noticed them at once, and some called out, but they were in a hurry. Mamako greeted them politely, but the party kept moving toward the Mom Shop.

"The town doesn't seem different," Mamako said. "Maybe this problem isn't as bad as it sounds?"

"Let's hope not. But we still gotta fix things before they get worse. Here we are!"

They burst into the Mom Shop like they owned the place.

Behind the counter was the girl who ran the shop for them—Mone. Seated at the table was a mother with a young boy. It seemed Mone was busy seeing to them.

"Oh, Masato! Everyone! You came!"

"Uh, yeah...didn't mean to interrupt, though. Bad timing?"

"Not at all! It's actually perfect timing. Maaasaaatooo!"

Mone threw herself into Masato's arms, as nimble as a small animal. Her face melted into a puddle of happiness, and she rubbed it against his chest. "Rub, rub!" "Hey!" The mother at the table was staring at them, mouth agape.

Everyone else seemed used to this. Mamako smiled. Porta smiled. And...

"Yeah, yeah, typical." Wise seemed unbothered.

"Wonders never cease." Medhi seemed exasperated.

"I really feel like you guys could stand to act a *little* jealous," Masato grumbled. "Whatever—settle down, Mone! You're on the job, remember? Not the time to make me dote on you."

"Just a minute! I need to recharge! Things are getting real bad and I'm sooo tired!"

"You mean this rapid child growth thing? We're here because of the quest you posted..."

"Right, that! The customer here is one of them! Let me introduce you."

Mone snapped back into work mode and pulled the party over to the customers.

The mother had brought her four-year-old son to the Mom Shop. She hopped up, greeting Mamako, going for the handshake—judging from her excitement level, she was obviously a fan. But her enthusiasm soon faded away.

She was clearly very worried about her son.

"If I could read better, Mommy wouldn't need to read to me... I gotta...work harder! 'Once...upon...a time...'"

The little boy was looking unusually stressed for a four-year-old, scowling at a picture book on the table, reading out loud as he copied the words onto a different piece of paper.

He was so focused on his studying that he seemed oblivious to his surroundings.

"Uh, he seems like a real go-getter?"

"He is, he really is. But..." The mother frowned. Then she sat down next to her son. "You've been working so hard! Time for a little break. How about a snack?"

"No, I'm good."

"You mean...you don't need a snack?"

"If I get hungry, I'll get something to eat."

"Y-you will? Then what's Mommy supposed to do?"

"You don't need to do anything, Mommy. If I can do something myself, I'll do it. I need to work harder so I can do everything by myself, so don't bother me, okay?"

"R-right...sorry..." The mother pulled back, looking ever so sad. "It's always like this now. Just the other day he was always begging for my help and attention. I could barely peel him off me! But now..."

"He just suddenly changed? Weird," said Wise.

"An independent streak developing this suddenly and this dramatically is clearly unnatural," remarked Medhi.

"Yes...if he had just grown up naturally, I would be delighted, but... it all happened so fast that I got worried and decided I should get help here."

"Yeah, this definitely seems like a problem."

"Right...and this isn't the only report I've had," Mone said. She ran to the counter and came back with a stack of documents.

Each contained a summary of consultations the Mom Shop had received. In addition to statements taken from mothers in person, there were others that had letters attached to them—over fifty documents in all.

"This entire pile is all the same kind of thing. The first one was about a week ago…and they've been coming in faster and faster."

"Maman Village…Mahweh…Thermo…Yomamaburg…Myma…and Materville. Reports from all around the world."

"Yeah…this is definitely weird, right? Something must be going on."

"I agree," Masato said. "But we'll have to think about it later. Only one thing we should do right here and now. Solve the problem in front of us."

Even with the entire party together, if they couldn't do anything about this issue, the world-famous Mom Shop's reputation would plummet. They needed to get to the bottom of this.

Seeing Masato so determined made the little boy's mother tear up. Mamako looked ready to cry with her.

Wise and Medhi just looked confused.

"Yo, you two! What's with the sour expressions?" Masato demanded of Wise and Medhi.

"It's just, like… You suddenly developed leadership? And that's, like…ew."

"Ew, how? What's wrong with that?! You should be glad!"

"This must be more unnatural growth! It is totally unlike Masato."

"I've just been taking my time to grow and develop! One step at a time! It's not at all unnatural!"

"Ma-kun's all grown up… He can do anything now… He doesn't need Mommy any more. *Sniff.*"

"You, too, Mom? This is no time to goof off! Let's focus!"

"Hee-hee-hee. You're right, I'm sorry. But don't worry! Our hardest worker is already investigating."

"Bwuh?! She beat me to it?!"

While they'd been squabbling, one party member had taken action: Porta.

"Um…do you want something?" the boy asked.

"I'm investigating if there's anything strange about you! Please don't mind me!"

"Uh…okay…"

Porta had sat down opposite the boy, and was looking him over intently, like a lot was riding on this.

"It's a waste not to be spoiled when you have the chance… Your mommy won't always be with you. So…hnggg!"

Her keen, Appraise skill–oriented eyes activated, and she stared at the boy so intently, he couldn't concentrate at all. This continued for a full minute.

And then Porta found it.

"Can I see that kitty-cat pin you've got on your chest?"

"Huh? This? Hmm…well, you're not Mommy, so I guess it's okay."

The pin had an adorable cat's face on it. The boy unpinned it and handed it to Porta.

Immediately afterward…

"Mm…wow, I'm sooo hungry… Mommy! I'm hungry!"

"Huh? Oh, of course! You want a snack?"

"Yes! I do! Gimme a snack!"

"You want a snack now? Should Mommy get you one? You're done studying?"

"I don't wanna study! I want a snack from Mommy!"

The boy's expression loosened and he threw his arms around his mom's leg. "Mm!" he started rubbing his cheek on it, then took her hand, yanked it back and forth a minute, and then attached himself to her leg again.

This sudden transformation shocked his mother. She looked up at the party.

They stared back at her, equally shocked.

"Uh…huh?"

"He's suddenly super spoiled…"

"Y-yes…this is how he used to be. He hates studying but loves clinging to me. This is what my son is supposed to be like!"

"So, he's suddenly back to normal…which means…"

"The cause of his sudden maturation was that pin?"

All eyes turned to the pin in Porta's hands.

Porta had been Appraising it carefully. She nodded.

"Yes! I think this is the cause! Look here!"

Engraved in tiny letters on the back of the pin near the edge was: © 20xx Libere Rebellion.

In accordance with the Universal Copyright Convention, they had claimed their full rights as creators to produce a perfectly legal product.

"Thanks to them being sticklers for the most pointless things, this mystery has been easily solved."

"So basically, it's the usual suspects."

"Forcing children to mature early, urging them to become independent of their parents, making mothers unhappy. That's their plan, huh? Seems to be a form of brainwashing."

"Similar to the effect those dark stones had. We smashed the machine that made those back at their base, but I guess they found a new way. It's like playing Whac-A-Mole. So how did he get this?"

Masato glanced at the mother, but she just shook her head, clearly at a loss.

So only the boy himself would know. Mamako knelt down before him, smiling.

"Hi there! Can you tell me something? Who gave you that pin?"

"Santa did! I woke up in the morning and it was left on my windowsill!"

So three Santas in black Rebellion coats were searching for houses where children lived and leaving pins behind. That sounded like a *lot* of work.

"Hey, look at this! I think the other problem children might have pins, too!"

"Seriously?"

Mone had been checking over her other documentation. She passed it around, and the many statements mentioned pins with animal faces on them.

"'My daughter is wearing a pin I've never seen before, and when I try to take it off, she flies into a rage,'" Masato read from one of the statements. "This one…and this one, too? That settles it."

"The pins are behind it," said Wise. "If we confiscate those, the problem goes away. Time to take action."

"The documents all have their addresses, so we should start by at least collecting the ones in Catharn," suggested Medhi.

"I'll make a public warning notice and have it posted all over the world!" Mone said. "That should take care of the rest of the pins!"

"Right, then…," Masato began.

"Everyone, be caref—" Mamako started to talk over him like she always did, but…

"Let's gather the bad pins! I'll do my best!" Porta was even more enthusiastic.

"Y-yeah…," Masato said.

Porta was already running out the door, so everyone else hastily scrambled to their feet and gave chase.

Masato's party split up to cover more houses in less time.

"Hello, Mom Shop!"

"Hi, there! How can I help you, suspicious man?"

"I'm not suspicious! Don't call the cops, okay?!"

The bossy little girl who answered the door had a rabbit pin on her chest. This could prove to be a thorny interaction, but Masato had locked on to the first recovery target.

At another house, so had Wise.

"Mwah-ha-ha! Cute pin ya got there! Can I take a look?"

"Mm…sure, but who are you, ma'am?"

"Ma'am—?! …N-No, never mind, at your age I must look way older. Rrgh…"

Wise forced herself to lower the shaking fist she'd raised. Pin recovery still seemed likely.

Meanwhile, at another house, Medhi was growling, "Fork over that pin if you know what's good for you!"

"E-eeek! You can have it!"

The child immediately sensed the depths of her terrifying dark power and held out the pin willingly. Easily recovered! One down.

But while the teens were handling their tasks well, Mamako was struggling.

"You're somebody's mom, right? You can't have it!"

"Oh, don't be like that! Won't you let me see it for just a moment?"

"No! Go away!"

It seemed like the children had been manipulated to reject mothers—all of them refused to respond to Mamako's requests. "Oh dear…" "I'm so sorry…" Mamako was left exchanging apologetic looks with the children's own mothers.

But the most impressive performance by far was Porta's.

"Can I have that pin?"

"Okay! I don't mind if you take it. Here!"

At each house, she instantly made contact with the child and easily recovered the pin. She was already on her fourth!

She'd recovered her entire allotment.

"Mission complete! I did it!" she said, pumping her fist as she left the last house. Feeling very satisfied, she went back the way she'd come.

The party had agreed to meet up at the Mom Shop once they'd collected their pins.

Porta had intended to head directly there, but...

"...Oh, that's..."

...her path had taken her past the Catharn capital's Adventurers Guild.

This was where Porta had first met Masato and Mamako. It was a lovely place—the start of their adventures together.

But she had other things on her mind right now.

"......!"

Porta took a quick look around her and then hid in the shadows of the building.

Making sure no one could see her, she pulled a crumpled piece of paper out of her bag, spreading it out.

It was the posting she'd found at the town guild and quickly hidden.

Specifically, it was a wanted poster asking for information leading to the arrest of a certain criminal.

The picture included was very realistic, like they'd just xeroxed a photograph.

It showed a woman in glasses, eyes downcast, looking tired, face turned slightly away from the camera. She appeared to be in her mid-thirties.

Porta knew this "criminal" well. Better than anyone else in the world.

"I wonder if it's posted at this guild, too? In that case...!"

She had to recover it before anyone else could see. Otherwise, someone might capture the person on the poster.

Porta slipped out of the shadows and dashed into the guild.

She made a beeline for the bulletin board. "...ah!" The poster *was* on display, but she managed to recover it without anyone seeing...

Well, except for the receptionist.

"Oh, wait! That's...!"

"Eep?! E-er, I didn't take anything! Pardon me!"

"I said wait! We were told not to post that—oh, she's gone."

Porta had not stopped to listen.

She moved quickly to a deserted area, desperately, blindly trying to wipe the tears that wouldn't stop flowing…until she was safely back in the shadows.

Her heart was pounding like she'd done something bad. It was awful. But she tried to convince herself she'd had no choice.

"N-now what? I don't know what to do…"

She stared down at the face on the page, thinking. Her thoughts were already a mess, but she had to make up her mind or…

Just then, she noticed something swaying out of the corner of her eye. The little doll that hung from her bag.

"…Oh, right! I have this!"

Having remembered something important, Porta clutched her bag tightly and ran off.

Porta sprinted until she reached a field outside the Catharn capital.

She was a noncombatant, so the monsters did not register her as an enemy. They just watched in confusion as she dashed past them.

She was headed for the plateau overlooking the city, where the transport point was. This was a special point that allowed you to pass through an area known as the Transport Palace, connecting to the real world or to the worlds on other servers.

"I'm sure I can contact her here! I'll get in touch, talk a bit, and hurry back to the Mom Shop! It'll be fine!"

Porta raced up the stairs, reaching the transport point and the mystic pillars that surrounded it.

She immediately put the doll, Piita, to use.

"Here goes! Ready…hah!"

Porta tugged on Piita's legs.

Suddenly, an earsplitting alarm sounded.

"This should do it! If she knows there's an emergency…"

Pii! Pii! Pii!

"…she'll come and check on it…I think…"

Pii! Pii! Pii!

"Uh…that's so loud…"

Figuring the signal must have been received by now, Porta tugged on the doll's arms, and the sound stopped. The legs switched it on, and the arms switched it off—like a child distress alarm. Now then.

She just had to wait.

"...Ah! She came!"

A ball of blinding light descended from the sky and onto the transport point. The person she'd been waiting for had arrived. Porta ran over, ecstatic...

But.

"We finally get away from Hahako, and now there's an emergency summons? My head's spinning with everything we're juggling already, jeez."

"You never responded to any of our caaaalls, but now you call uuuuus? Who do you think you aaaare?"

"Y'all just remember we're only here 'cause we're obligated to be. This better be worth...mm?"

As the light dissipated, three figures were revealed.

Fierce as a tiger, radiating indignation—Anti-Mom Amante.

Gazing languidly at her through her bangs, toying with a bone-shaped accessory—Scorn-Mom Sorella.

And with a sharklike hood pulled low over her face, spitting words in a manly tone, the bleary-eyed Fighter—Frighten-Mom Fratello.

Three of the Four Heavenly Kings of the Libere Rebellion appeared!

Porta's jaw dropped, astonished.

"Uh...wahhhh...?!"

"What in tarnation? It's Porta, y'all."

"You're right. What's she doing here?"

"Heeey! Long time no seeee, Porta... Is it just youuuuu?"

"Y-yes! I'm the only one here! Ohhh, this is no time to answer...um, um...whaaa?!"

Porta had definitely not been calling *them*. Never.

But here they were anyway, getting closer.

Porta took a step backward, but they took three steps closer.

"We're officially enemies, but we have no intention of harming you, Porta. Don't worry. Do you mind answering some questions?"

"Were you the one who called uuuus?"

"N-no! I didn't call you!"

"Yer the only person here. Who else coulda? This don't make a lick of sense. We got a call on the Rebellion emergency broadcast... Wait, now hold on just one darn minute!"

"Huh? Oh...!"

Porta had backed all the way to the edge of the cliff, and one foot slipped off the edge.

Fratello's hands shot out, but too late—Porta went over the edge, falling...!

But then, a dark swirl appeared behind her. A hand emerged from within it, catching Porta's back.

"...H-huh?"

"Humph. There you are, Master."

"Er...Master? The leader of the Libere Rebellion...?"

"Mm. That there's our boss. Only the Master can operate them dark swirly things. Ain't no doubt about it."

The hand pushed Porta safely back onto the plateau, and a person stepped out of the swirl.

It was a woman just starting to show signs of age. She was clad in jet-black armor, with the Rebellion's trademark coat over it.

The eyes behind her glasses looked exhausted. They were staring at the ground, never once meeting Porta's gaze.

The intense gloom on her face combined with her dreary getup made her look like the ruler of the underworld—however...

"Oh! Mommy!"

""""......Huh?""""

...Porta would know her anywhere. The woman from the dark swirl was Porta's mother.

Now it was the Four Heavenly Kings whose mouths hung open.

"Hold on...wh-what?"

"This woman...is Porta's moooom? B-But...if she can use the swiiiirls...she's also our Maaaster? What does that meeean?"

"I ain't never met her in the flesh before, neither... Porta! Fill us in here, would ya?"

"Er, um, I'm also confused! But this is my mommy!" Porta said with a huge smile.

Then she ran over with the wanted poster.

"Mommy! I found this and was so shocked that I decided to summon you! I'm sure it's all a big mistake, but I was so worried... Oh...!"

Without a word, Porta's mother had grabbed the poster from her, crumpled it up, and flung it away.

Not even glancing at her daughter, she addressed the Heavenly Kings.

"I'll explain what is needed. But not here. We must move before the Hero's Mother or Hahako sense something amiss. Come."

"Y-yeah...if Porta's here, Mamako Oosuki must be nearby. And that awful Hahako..."

"I guess...we go with herrr?"

"Mm. I'm fixin' for an explanation 'bout your identity, and for abandoning us all in Materland. Nothing ventured, nothing gained."

Porta's mother turned on her heel and vanished into the swirl. The three Heavenly Kings followed cautiously.

Only Porta was left behind.

"Er, um...Mommy? What should I—?"

"Go back to your friends," a cold voice replied. The swirl began to vanish.

Porta bit her lip, wiped the tears welling up, and tried to think.

Should she run after her mother and jump into the swirl?

Or go back to Catharn and her party?

She wavered between the two options for a moment—then made up her mind.

The sun was setting. It would soon be night.

Masato's party had gathered at the Mom Shop a long time ago.

Sitting at the table, Masato dragged his eyes way from his long-since-empty teacup and looked around.

Mamako was sitting next to him, being very quiet. Wise was across from him, staring at the ceiling. Next to her was Medhi, staring out the window.

Mone was behind the counter, organizing paperwork.

One party member was missing.

"...She's way too late. I'm gonna go look for her."

"Yes. Mommy's coming, too."

Wise and Medhi both stood up as well. The four of them left Mone to watch the shop in case Porta returned, and they headed for the door.

But as they did, the doorbell rang.

"Oh! She's finally back...?"

Everyone looked.

Someone was attempting to push a giant bundle through the door. It was too big and was stuck in the doorframe, so they weren't making much progress, but were doing a decent job of brute-forcing it.

"Hngg...I shoulda turned it the other way around... I made a real darn mess of this..."

"Uh...I know that voice... Fratello?!"

"That you, sonny? How goes it? Hate to ask, but can y'all gimme a hand with this? You pull on that end... Oh, there it goes! Mahhh!"

"Whoa, stop! What even is this thing? It's not dangerous, is it?!"

The black-cloaked Santas behind the earlier pin-cident could well be bringing disaster directly to the Mom Shop. Masato tried to push the package back outside—but was too late.

The cloth around the package came undone, and the contents came tumbling out. "Crap!" "Ma-kun?!" They all fell on Masato's head.

But he was unharmed. The impact was extremely soft.

"Uh...what are these?"

There was something resting on his head. He picked it up and saw it was a triangular piece of cloth.

Women's underwear. With green stripes.

"I've seen these before... Oh, I know! They're Wise's Thursday panties!"

"What? For real?! ...Whoa, you're right, these *are* mine."

"I knew it! You wrote a *W* on the tag to avoid getting them mixed up with Medhi's. She put an *M*."

"Yep. But if you get it upside-down, they look the same, so it hasn't really helped... Wait, why do *you* know any of this?"

"I was thinking the same thing. You're too well informed."

"L-look, they just got mixed in with my laundry once and I happened to catch a glimpse! No malicious intent, I swear!"

Intent didn't seem to matter. Both girls were advancing on him, smiling from ear to ear. "Gah?!" A magic tome hit the side of his face. "Urgh!" A staff rapped the top of his head. Masato was no longer unharmed.

There were a lot of ordinary household things lying around him. Not just underwear; pajamas, school uniforms, swimsuits. Cooking supplies, too; rice, miso, soy sauce...

"My spare clothes, Mom's costume collection...ingredients we use every day...this is our luggage, right?"

"Mm. It's all your things, sonny! Came here to return them to y'all."

"Return…no, wait! Porta was carrying these for us! You didn't…do something to her, did you?!"

Masato scrambled to his feet, drawing his sword. Wise, Medhi, and even Mamako all braced themselves, looking tense. "I'll, uh…evacuate!" Mone hid behind the counter.

Fratello just gave them all a dazed look, then held her hands up.

"…What's the meaning of this?"

"I ain't here to fight, sonny. Y'all're jumping to conclusions. We ain't done a thing to Porta."

"I don't believe that for a second."

"Then y'all will have to take her word for it."

Fratello turned and left. "Wait!" The party ran out of the Mom Shop in pursuit.

Outside, they found not just Fratello, but Amante and Sorella as well.

"You guys, too? The Heavenly Kings out in force?"

"Heh-heh…that's right. The Four Heavenly Kings have assembled at last."

"The heck are you sounding all high-and-mighty about?" said Wise.

"If something happened, we certainly wouldn't mind you just explaining it," added Medhi.

"Don't be stupid, no reason I'd…"

"Oh, ohhh! I think rather than have Amante explaaaaain, it would be better if she just came oooout. Come, cooome!"

Amante and Sorella stepped aside, opening a path between them.

A tiny figure stepped forward.

Dressed in a long black Rebellion coat, with a bag slung over her shoulder…

…was Porta, looking extremely stressed.

"Uh…wait…Porta, why are you…huh?"

"Please listen to me!" she said, bowing her head. "Masato, Mama, Wise, Medhi—thank you for everything! I'm now the Fourth Heavenly King of the Libere Rebellion! I'm…she who loves moms, Praise-Mom Porta!"

Porta had left the party and turned to the dark side.

"Uh…no, hang on… Porta, this is a joke, right?" asked Wise.

"It's true! I'm one of the Four Heavenly Kings! I'm now in a party with Amante, Sorella, and Fratello!"

"This doesn't make sense! It just can't be possible…," said Medhi.

"Oh, I know—it's the pin, right? You've been brainwashed by the Rebellion's schemes! Amante, explain."

"Pins? Brainwashing? I have no idea what you're talking about."

"Don't play dumb now, Amante!" shouted Masato. "This is your moment to just blab everything! That's your role in life!"

"How rude! I've never once just blabbed anything! I don't remember getting assigned that role ever!"

"Sure, suuuure, you don't even realize you're doing iiiit. Just shut up, okaaay?"

"Y'all need to calm down. I know this is a helluva shock, but we legitimately have no idea what you're talking about, ya hear? We ain't brainwashing nobody."

They really didn't seem to know anything about the pins. That didn't make sense...but there was no time to press the point.

"I've returned all your things! I've said my good-byes! I'll be going back to the Rebellion castle now!"

Porta took out an item with the word GO carved into it—a jewel with a transport spell effect.

"Wait, Porta! I said wait!"

"I won't wait! Forgive me! Good-bye!"

"Porta, dear! Please, wait! ...At least tell us one thing!"

"Mama...wh-what is it?"

"Do you not want to be with us anymore? Is that why you joined the Four Heavenly Kings?"

"That's not true! I love all of you! But I...I want to be with my real mommy more! So...!"

She held the jewel aloft. Porta and the other three Heavenly Kings were encased in a cocoon of light, which rocketed up into the night sky.

"With her mom...? What does that mean...?" Masato asked.

But no one knew the answer. The rest of the party stared wordlessly into the sky as the light of the spell faded from view.

Porta had been in their party since their adventure began. Always at their side. And in the blink of an eye...

...Porta was gone.

Mom Roster Profile 1
Mamako Oosuki

■Age:
How old do I look? Hee-hee-hee.

■Hobbies:
Keeping records of Ma-kun's growth!

■Specialties:
I suppose cooking and laundry count.

■Best Feature:
I've been told I have a lovely smile.

■Childhood Dream:
I wanted to be a witch after watching
an anime about one.

■Catchphrase:
"I'm Ma-kun's mommy." All I have to do
is chant those words, and I feel myself
getting even stronger!

■Child-Rearing Philosophy:
I've never really thought about it.
Just make every day fun and healthy.
And get along with your child. That's
all I wish for.

■To Your Beloved Child:
Dear Ma-kun,
    Thank you for going on an adventure with Mommy. I'm having so much fun every day!
Are you having fun, too? I hope we have many more wonderful adventures together.
From the mother who loves you more than anything.

Chapter 2 The One You Always Say "Good Morning" To Is Gone. What Now? The Answer's Obvious.

The castle had no windows, allowing no sunlight to enter.

It was the ghouls that announced the arrival of morning; spectral creatures who'd long since abandoned their flesh. They roamed the castle halls, tapping the magic stones that lined them, summoning a soft white glow.

They could pass through the walls at will, even lighting up the private bedrooms.

"...Mm...huh? Whaaa?! A g-g-g-ghost?!"

Porta's eyes opened at the light and found a ghoul directly in front of her.

The ghoul seemed unconcerned with Porta's shock. It vanished through a nearby wall.

"Th-that was spooky..."

But she was definitely awake now. Time to get up.

She clambered out from beneath the stuffed animals piled atop her very soft bed. First things first: time to wash her face.

There was a sink on the wall, and she ran over to it.

"Ooooh, it's so cold! But that also helps wake me up!"

With her face clean, she now needed to get changed. She dashed to the closet at the far end of the room. It was a very big room.

She changed from her animal pajamas to her Four Heavenly Kings coat.

"And I've got my shoulder bag with me... Time to eat!"

The Libere Rebellion didn't bother eating breakfast together.

There was a table in the center of the dining room and trays lined up on it, each with a breakfast platter. Maybe the ghouls got it ready? Each had toast, ham, eggs, potato salad, and soup.

It looked good, but it seemed like it had been sitting out for a while.

"I guess I must've overslept! That's my fault! ...Okay, then, thanks for the food! ...Mm! That's delicious!"

She took a bite of cold toast and a sip of similarly cold soup.

Her cheery voice echoed through the vast room.

She focused on her food, hunched over, staring only at the tray.

There was no need to look up. There was no one else around her.

"…I'll be fine. When I first came to the game world, I always ate alone like this, so I'm fine," she told herself.

But then her hands paused.

She went and got four stuffed animals from her bed, set them up next to her, and finished her breakfast.

The plans for the day had been communicated the night before. They started with a meeting.

Once she was ready, Porta headed to the throne room, where they'd agreed to meet. "G-good morning!" she said, greeting the Skeleton Knights who lined the passage. The castle was huge, and it took her a while to get there.

But finally, she reached a giant set of doors with the Rebellion logo on them.

"Um…good morning! It's Porta! Can I come in?" she called. Then she waited.

The door opened a crack, and Amante poked her head out.

"You don't need to ask, y'know. You're one of the Four Heavenly Kings, Porta. Just get in here!"

"R-right! Thank you! Pardon me!"

Amante's words were harsh, but Porta caught a hint of kindness behind them, and that was enough to cheer her up.

Everyone but Porta was already assembled. "Moooornin'!" Sorella called with a languid wave of her hand. Fratello just grunted and held out a fist.

They'd been enemies a day before but seemed totally comfortable with Porta being there.

She was relieved, and the strain on her face eased…

"You're late. Not that it matters."

This voice completely shattered the laid-back vibe.

It came from the person on the throne at the top of the stairs— looming over them like a demon lord.

She wore a suit of armor with a coat over that; her chin rested in her hand, and her eyes stared into the distance, as if she could not even be bothered to look at her minions. A very solitary, aloof demon lord.

"Um...M-Mommy...good m—"

"If you have important business to discuss, keep it brief."

Was a morning greeting "important business"? ...Didn't seem to be. Porta shut her mouth and stared at the ground.

The other three Heavenly Kings immediately gathered around her. "Er...?" Sorella had given her a big hug from behind. Fratello silently stood with her back to Porta, as if guarding her.

Amante gave Porta a pat on the shoulder and glared up at the throne. "Master, I have a proposal."

"You may speak."

"This is the first time we've all been together. Perhaps we should all introduce ourselves."

"Unnecessary. I know who you all are."

"That may be true, but we don't know who *you* are. So..."

"I am the creator and operator of the Libere Rebellion. My name... As a mother who, in death, descended to the underworld, I shall call myself Dark-Mom Deathmother."

She had clearly made that up on the spot, likely based on the castle's ghoulish interior.

Amante appeared displeased.

"I didn't mean just your name. I was looking for a clear declaration of whether you're actually Porta's mom or not."

"Legally speaking, I suppose so."

"Legally...? What kind of phrasing is that? Is that the best you can do? In front of your own daughter?!"

"I'm fine!" Porta said, tugging Amante's coat. She shook her head vigorously, showing she didn't mind.

"You're not fine! How could you..."

"Amanteee...that's enough for nooow."

"Time to listen. Shut yer trap."

"......All right, fine."

With Sorella and Fratello both against her, Amante reluctantly dropped the subject.

Dark-Mom Deathmother did not even bother glancing at the commotion her statement had provoked.

"Since your business is concluded, I will issue instructions. Begin by shoring up this castle's defenses. Immediately."

"The defeeenses? Who's going to attaaaack? Oh, riiiight…you've got a wanted poster circulaaating."

"Sure, but this castle ain't somewhere people can just get to. Ain't nobody comin' here."

"The Admins are the ones after me. They have the power to change these settings… And even if a problem is beyond an Admin's abilities, there are certain people who can step in and solve it through the most extreme means."

""""Oh…"""""

Everyone knew from personal experience who *that* was.

"Sooner or later, they'll get here. I can't have that happening too soon. I need time to ensure my plan does not go unfinished. Which means you must promptly…"

"Yes! I can make lots of traps so that nobody gets close to you, Mommy! Leave it to me!"

Porta enthusiastically threw her hand up, seizing the opportunity.

Dark-Mom Deathmother raised an eyebrow, as if mildly surprised. But this still did not prompt her to look at Porta.

"…I believe I was clear it is your friends who will be attacking."

"Yes!" Porta said, even more enthusiastically. "I know them well, so I think I can stop them! I'm one of the Four Heavenly Kings now, so I'll do my part!"

"Very well…then do what you think best."

"Okay! Um…I, Praise-Mom Porta, will protect you, Mommy! Just you watch!"

Upon stating her full title, Porta turned on her heel and dashed out of the throne room.

Dark-Mom Deathmother didn't watch her go. She just stared absently into space.

Then she said, "I believe I gave that child a different name—she who mourns mothers, Post-Mom. What's this 'Praise-Mom' she speaks of?"

"Porta gave herself a new title. She's calling herself the one who loves moms."

"Personally, I wish she'd knock that oooooff."

"Mm. It don't fit with the Four Heavenly Kings shtick. Loving a mother like you is a sign Porta's got bats in her belfry."

"Silence."

Dark-Mom Deathmother's glare met Fratello's bleary gaze. Neither backed down.

"Oh? So you'll look me in the eye now, eh? ...So which bit ticked you off? 'A mother like you'? Or the part where I mocked Porta? You ain't done nothin' mom-like but you'll get mad on her behalf?"

"I said silence. We don't have time to waste on idle chitchat. All of you should get to work immediately. If you obey my orders without question, I shall overlook your insolence."

"What if I don't obey? You gonna dish out the punishments?"

"...Your manner displeases me. Who do you think you are?"

"Are you seriously asking that?"

"That's what weeee want to knoooow."

Amante and Sorella joined the staring contest between Fratello and Dark-Mom Deathmother.

"You've yet to fulfill your exposition obligations. You sank the Materland hideout into the ocean with us still in it. What were you thinking?"

"Management's analysis achieved results sooner than I'd expected. I was forced to take drastic action to avoid them securing evidence of my actions. Time was of the essence. I apologize for the lack of consideration."

"Theeeen, after thaaat, you didn't answer no matter how many times we caaaalled. Why nooooot?"

"Same reasons. I was focused on evading management's investigation. I didn't have the time to respond. Again, I apologize."

"Lip service apologies," Fratello grumbled.

"You have your explanations. Obey my instructions..."

"Don't be ridiculous."

All three of them stared up at Dark-Mom Deathmother, radiating hostility.

"I shouldn't even have to explain this, but I'll make this very clear. We find this treatment completely unacceptable. And we see no reason why we should follow you."

"My, my, such disobedient minions."

"Damn skippy. How else would we become the Four Kings rebelling against mothers?"

"We haaaate mothers. Why would we obey instructions from oooone?"

"I see. That is true. You're completely right. You are obeying the tenets of the Rebellion you joined. In which case, how's this?"

Dark-Mom Deathmother raised a hand.

Above her head appeared a shoulder bag far larger than Porta's, its mouth yawning like that of some giant beast.

An avalanche of weapons poured out. Swords, daggers, spears, and axes. They surrounded the three Heavenly Kings, tips pointed at their throats.

"That's…"

"My in-game job is Merchant. The bonus abilities provided to moms have given me unlimited weapons, armor, and items. And this is just one way I can use them."

"You can use anythiiiing?! That's not faaaair!"

"Settle down, Sorella. Even if she can use any weapon, it don't mean squat if she can't hit us. Right, Amante?"

"Ha-ha! Exactly. No attacks will work on me! All of these will bounce off—!"

"You think so?" Dark-Mom Deathmother proceeded to chant a spell: "*Trade-in.*"

Instantly, light drained from the Heavenly Kings' bodies—like the light of their souls.

And the light changed to dictionary-sized books, which vanished into the shoulder bag.

"Er…what was that…?"

"Reflection, debuffs, attack bonuses against mothers—I purchased each of your unique skills, converted to skill books."

"What are you talking abooout?! You can't buy skiiiiills!"

"Of course I can. I'm a Merchant. Literally everything can be traded. Oh, right! I have to pay for them. I'd value those skills at…this much."

Three 1 mum coins were spat out of her bag, rolling to the Heavenly Kings' feet.

"Ridiculous… Hey, Amante."

"Amanteeee!"

"Huh?"

Fratello punched Amante in the stomach. "Gah!" The attack landed. No reflection.

Sorella slapped Amante's face. "Ow!" The attack hit. No reflection.

"Wh-wh-what noooow? We've really lost our skiiiills!"

"Seems like it... I don't think it was necessary to test it *twice*, though."

"Anyways, we ain't got no way to fight. She's really done a number on us... So, what now? You got us under control, so we gotta follow your orders?"

"Exactly. You will obey me. Do your duty as the Rebellion's Four Heavenly Kings. Once you have fulfilled your duties, I shall return your skills. That is all."

The hovering weapons surrounding them parted, opening a path to the throne room door. A clear invitation to leave.

"...One final question, if you don't mind," said Amante. "Masato Oosuki mentioned something about pins and brainwashing. We'd never heard anything about that..."

"Currently I am personally heading up a stratagem to eliminate mothers from the world at large. This stratagem does not require your participation. Your help would doom it to failure, and I can't allow that."

"Ohhhh? We'd only screw it uuuup? In other words, you've already deemed us uselesssss."

"Fine by me. No skin off my nose. Humph!"

Blustering, the three Heavenly Kings left the room.

Dark-Mom Deathmother watched them go. No one saw her self-deprecating smile.

Once they'd left the throne room, all three Heavenly Kings sighed.

"...I still can't believe the Master is really Porta's mom. What a shock."

"I knoooow! I thought it was weird how she was so interested in Portaaaa, so I figured they were relaaaated, but...I didn't think she'd be her moooom."

"But why's her mom trying to erase all moms from the world? The heck is she thinkin'...?"

Fratello stopped in her tracks, staring back at the throne room door.

But her question went unanswered.

"I don't get why she treats Porta like that, either."

"Riiight? What kind of mom is like thaaat? Porta's trying to prove how much she loves her, but she won't even look her in the eeeeeye."

"Yet she was all prepared for her," said Fratello. "She's got a room and a custom-made Heavenly King coat. Speakin' of, there was a room just like it at the old hideout before it sank."

"Yeah…it's like she always meant for Porta to be one of the Four Heavenly Kings. But once she shows up, she's all indifferent. It makes me sick!"

An innocent Skeleton Knight, who just happened to be standing there, ended up getting his head punched off so Amante could vent.

But it wasn't really harmed by this. It was already dead, after all. The body just scrambled off to recover its head.

"My, myyyy. Aren't you angryyyy. I do sympathize, buuuut…"

"Ain't no point thinking about what we don't know. Times like this, it's best to keep things simple."

"…Yeah, good point," Amante said, releasing her frustration in a huge sigh. Then she laughed. "Heh-heh-heh. At the very least, we're clear the Master is a mother. And that she played us for fools. The worst kind of mother! Which means there's only one thing the Four Heavenly Kings should do next."

"Riiiight! What do we do when a mother pisses us ooooff?"

"We mess her up."

Sorella and Fratello exchanged malicious grins.

"If Porta's determined to protect that awful mother…well, I'd love to talk her out of it, but we'll have to leave that for later. First, we need to ruin the Master's plan."

"The Master seems concerned about who's coming to attack this caaaastle. Which meeeans…"

"We oughta bring 'em here."

"You can't reach this place via any normal means of transport, so we'll need to guide the one person she's afraid of… I don't suppose there's anyone capable of something that extreme just hanging around here, huh?"

Amante glared across the hall. There was nobody else there, but…

The floor began bubbling like molten sugar, gradually taking human form.

Mamako's face, Mamako's hair, and finally, Mamako's figure—in a black dress.

The unique creation modeled after Mamako—Hahako.

"How did you know? ...Oh, that's it! Parents and their children share a natural psychic bond! Hee-hee-hee."

"Nope. You've just been following us so relentlessly that I've somehow learned to sense when you're nearby. Anyway..."

"Yes, leave it to me!" said Hahako. "Porta's mother is most concerned about Mamako. I'll bring her and her party here."

"Heh-heh-heh, exactly, bring Mamako Oosuki...wait..."

"It's so nice of you to invite your former enemy over! When did you become friends? I think that's just lovely! Hee-hee-hee. I knew you were all good girls."

Hahako smiled happily and melted back into the floor.

"Uhhhh...the Master's enemiiiies...are the Rebellion's enemiiiies..."

"The same folks we've got our hackles up about..."

"And we just agreed to bring them here... Are we, like, actually dumb?"

The three of them stared at each other for a long moment.

"""".....We're *so* dumb......"""""

The answer was too obvious to deny, but no less depressing.

Meanwhile...

"...What does this mean?"

"It is exactly what it appears to be."

Masato was lying on the lap of the Mysterious Nun, Shiraaase. She was staring down at him.

The back of his head was preoccupied with the sensation of thighs. Thighs belonging to someone else's mother—Shiraaase had a five-year-old daughter.

......What is this? What's going on?

He needed to get to the bottom of this.

He was currently in a room at an inn in the Catharn capital.

Glancing around, he saw Wise and Medhi leaning against the wall, glaring down at him.

Everyone had woken up at the crack of dawn for an early breakfast, so it was still morning.

We want to go search for Porta, but have no idea where she might be...
They'd all settled down somewhere, dealing with their anxiety as best they could.

Masato had sprawled out on his bed, eyes tightly closed, praying for Porta's safety.

Yes...and then...

Mamako had called out, "Ma-kun, if you don't mind?" and lifted his head, sitting down next to him. He'd known she was going for the lap pillow.

She must have been worried about how much this was upsetting him.

Masato had decided it wasn't worth picking a fight about, and let her do it...but then the lap pillow didn't feel quite right, and when he'd opened his eyes...

"Should I clean your ears while I'm at it?"

...he'd found Shiraaase staring expressionlessly down at him.

Mamako was standing by the side of the bed, and judging from her apologetic smile, she'd been in on the ruse.

Now fully clued in, Masato slowly sat up.

"...Thanks, I guess."

"My! You took that in stride. I expected to get yelled at!"

"Not really in the mood. Sorry."

"I see...in that case...Masato, grit your teeth."

"Huh?"

Shiraaase raised a hand, and slapped Masato hard on the cheek.

Everyone gaped at her. Especially Masato.

"Masato! What's gotten into you? Wise, Medhi, this is no time to sulk! Get yourselves together!"

They'd never seen Shiraaase genuinely angry before. Even her expression was angry!

Her words got under their skin more than the pain or surprise. They could feel their deadened insides springing back to life.

"That's...right," Masato stammered. "Yeah!"

"We're not the type to just mope around!" said Wise.

"Moping doesn't change anyth—!" started Medhi.

"I've come to visit you, but not only did you fail to speak to me, you didn't even notice my arrival! Who do you think you are? Give me your undivided attention!"

"What?! *That's* what you're mad about?"

"Of course I am! I was sitting in a coffin outside the inn, waiting for you! Trying to fulfill my quota! But over an hour passed and no one came out to revive me!"

"There's no quota for showing up dead!"

"And! After all that waiting, I thought you'd finally brought me back, but it was just a total stranger! A random passing healer! I just assumed it was you, greeted you like always, and got, 'Uh...I don't know you...' like I was some sort of crazy person! That was super embarrassing! I was so embarrassed, I nearly died again!"

"I don't think you can blame that part on us..."

"Fair. I did jump to conclusions. Tee-hee."

Shiraaase was back to her usual blank expression. She rubbed Masato's cheek.

"I did my best to come up with a way to disperse the cloud of gloom that had settled over you...but raising my hand to you may have been ill-advised. I apologize."

"Your motives are pretty suspect, but...fine, it did snap me out of my funk."

"I must apologize to you, too, Mamako. I have done awful things to your precious son. I'm so sorry."

"No...honestly, it's my job to cheer Ma-kun up. I should have said something. But I just couldn't find it in me to scold him...you've been a great help."

"I see. I've helped you! Then I shall dwell on it no longer. I promise I will continue to be just as silly. Heh-heh-heh."

Not the best news, but irritation certainly drove away depression.

Everyone sat upright, facing Shiraaase.

"If you're here, you must have some critical infooormation, right? Lay it on us," said Masato.

"I'd be glad to. Mamako already told me all about Porta's desertion while you were all moping around like idiots."

"Phrasing! Not that I can deny it..."

"First, the reason Porta left the party...requires that I infooorm you about Porta's mother."

Shiraaase pulled a piece of paper out of her pocket it and placed it on a table. It was a wanted poster with a likeness of Porta's mother on it.

"This is Porta's mom...?"

"Her name is Saori Hotta. She is Porta's real mother...and a producer of *MMMMMORPG* (working title)."

"......Huh?"

Not a title he'd been expecting. Masato's mind went momentarily blank.

"Porta's mom is a producer on this game?! Seriously?"

"Seriously. Mom's Massively Maternal Multiplayer Making-up-with-Offspring RPG is primarily run by mothers, even lowly drones such as myself. The government agency that manages it saw this as a chance to increase employment opportunities for women...but in Hotta's case, she was hired purely on the basis of her experience and accomplishments. In other words, she earned the role of producer."

"She worked her way up to that level while raising a kid? Wow," marveled Wise.

"It must have taken considerable effort," said Medhi. "A mother and a producer...oh...come to think of it, the whole point of this game is that you're here with your mom, so is the reason Porta was playing all by herself...?"

"More or less. Her mother was in a position to make that sort of request. But Hotta...was also doing terrible things behind the scenes, leading to our current predicament." Shiraaase tapped the wanted poster. "She had secretly created an in-game society dedicated to eliminating mothers from the game world. That society...is the Libere Rebellion."

Everyone gasped.

"Hotta is the mastermind behind the Rebellion...and once management discovered this, they attempted to take her in for questioning. But they were a moment too late, and Hotta fled into the game world, hiding herself here."

Porta's mother was the Rebellion leader. She was hiding somewhere inside the game.

"At that point, I should have immediately approached you...but I was delayed by the need to implement stopgaps against this sort of thing happening again and meetings planning our next actions. For her child to see a posting like this...well, that was certainly careless of us. I'm rather angry about it, honestly."

Porta had found the wanted poster, got in touch with her mother somehow, and gone to her side.

And decided to join the Libere Rebellion—to be with her mother.

"I see…so that's what she was hiding at the Adventurers Guild…it all makes sense now."

Masato let himself fall backward onto the bed.

He stared up at the ceiling, mulling it over.

"Porta's the only one who never got to travel with her mother…she must have missed her."

"Masato and Mamako were together the whole time, and both Medhi and I at least started out that way… Porta was always alone. Of course she'd get homesick."

"Even if her mother is the mastermind behind everything…especially if she was in trouble, she'd want to be with her, to help her however she could."

"Yes…Porta is such a nice girl. She would listen to her feelings and go running right to her mother's side. Knowing that is actually something of a relief!"

Mamako smiled gently and rubbed Masato's head. "Stop it!"

"Hee-hee-hee. Sorry." Perhaps she was wishing her own child would listen to his feelings more.

Seeing this demonstration of family bonds made everyone smile…

"But that resolves nothing. There are so many problems remaining," Shiraaase pointed out.

Their smiles faded.

"Right…even if parent-child reunions are a good thing, if the mom's like that…well, we can't just leave them to it and hope for the best." Masato hopped to his feet. "Sitting around thinking about it won't get us anywhere. We'd better go meet with Porta and her mom."

"It's the only way! We gotta talk it over, figure it out! Charge on in and see where it gets us!"

"Let's make a formal thing out of it. We certainly shouldn't show up empty-handed…"

"Right! Gotta prepare for the worst, make sure our equipment's in order…"

"You can't go to a meeting like that without a tray full of sweets. We'll have to make enough for the Four Heavenly Kings as well, so… maybe two boxes' worth?"

"Yo, Mom, what are you talking about? We're not raiding an enemy lair with boxes of sweets."

"Also," Shiraaase mentioned, "do you have any idea how to get where they are?"

They all just grinned.

"That's easy, Shiraaase."

"Yep. 'Cause since you showed up here…"

"You must already know where they—"

"But I don't?" Shiraaase said, blinking.

""""……Uh?""""

"I really don't," she insisted. "I'm aware the situation calls for swift action, but the world doesn't always make things that easy."

"True enough…"

"That said, you are the hero's party. Thinking for yourself, struggling to progress, and finally achieving a breakthrough—all part of a heroic adventure. Are you sure you wish to rely on help from others, always taking the easy path? Is that what you want, Masato?"

She had a very valid point.

Masato bit his lip, ashamed he'd ever wanted help.

"You're right… We should solve this ourselves."

"Well, that's easily said, but I've actually already made arrangements. I'm sure she'll be here soon…oh, and so she is."

"Huh?"

The floor in the corner of the room suddenly swelled up, taking a form that was the spitting image of Mamako.

"Oh, Hahako?!"

"Hello. Did I time that right?"

"Couldn't have been better. You got results?"

"I did. Just as you requested, Ms. Shiraaase, I have discovered Porta's mother's location. Porta was there, too. I can guide you all to her immediately. What do you say?"

Hahako smiled at Masato.

"Hoo boy…all that crap she talked, but she'd actually already set things up… You're sneaky, Shiraaase. In a good way, I guess."

"Just my way of making up for management's failings. Consider it my apology."

"Very well. Then we'll be happy to accept Hahako's offer."

"Oh, also—Masato, now that you've experienced the joys of another mother's lap pillow, I can offer you the unique title: Mom's Lap Pillow Master."

"Do not want!" *Denied!*

You give Shiraaase the slightest compliment and she'd immediately gets carried away. He turned his back on her and started getting his things together.

"Well, then, shall we? Everybody ready?" asked Hahako.

"Yes. I've got both boxes of cookies right here!"

"Mom's seriously bringing cookies…but maybe that's for the best! As long as her hands are full of sweets, she can't hold any weapons!"

"And we'll have to take care of any combat! Perfect," said Wise.

Just in case, they made sure everyone was carrying a good supply of healing potions, and it was time to go.

"Well, everyone, do take care."

"You aren't coming, Ms. Shiraaase?" Mamako asked.

"I shall remain here and handle the matter of the rapid child growth. Mone has had the warning posted everywhere, but that alone won't solve the crisis."

"Oh, right! I forgot about that," said Wise. "Geez, so many problems…"

"If you handle the root cause, everything else will sort itself out. So…"

"Very well. We'll both do what we can," said Masato. "Here we go!"

Countless white hands reached out of the floor, wrapped around them, and dragged them back down.

This was an ability only Hahako could use—as a creation of the game itself, she could submerge into the game's raw data. "What…is this…?" "It feels like sinking into a bottomless swamp!" The new sensation made the group's faces turn white as a sheet.

Shiraaase waited until the hero's party could be seen no more, and then let out a brief sigh.

"Right, then I'd better spring into action. First things first: swing by the Mom Shop and share information with Mone."

Shiraaase promptly departed the inn.

But the moment she stepped outside…

"Oh…?"

…the ground beneath her feet tilted upward, and she began sliding down it.

The road outside the inn had a depression in it—a crater. And Shiraaase was sliding into it.

"Uh-oh…"

"Oh, nun lady, you okay? I got a rope here! Grab on!"

A man in a fishmonger's apron was passing by, and he pulled her out.

"Thank you. That was quite helpful. But what is this?"

"I'm not really sure, but they're happening all over! The ground just suddenly *depresses*. Just like this."

"That's…very odd…"

"Definitely one word for it. Oh, come to think of it, this morning when I went to lay in my fish supply, there was a depression like this in the ocean, too. Smaller, but like…a section of the water was just…not there."

"I…find it hard to imagine a depression in the ocean."

"Maybe I'm just seeing things. But make sure you watch your step!"

The man laughed and walked away.

"Hmm. Most bizarre. Another mysterious phenomenon? Well, they say if you chase two hares, you'll catch neither. As planned, I'll handle the rapid child growth first."

For now, she would just make a mental note of this other strange occurrence.

Shiraaase turned toward the Mom Shop… "Oh…?" …and started sliding again. A second depression had opened silently next to her.

Proof the situation was getting steadily out of control.

Masato's party was moving rapidly.

"Like a walk through the ocean…swimming through a sea of data… does that sound right?"

"Strictly speaking, more like deep-sea diving…," replied Medhi. "It's pitch-black and we can't see anything."

"Well, yeah, there's nothing here but data," said Wise.

They were passing through a realm composed entirely of data—a realm beneath the game world.

Naturally, there were no shapes, colors, or anything else displayed.

"It's like being behind a set…like we've been shown just how fake the game world really is. Not ideal, but…we'll just have to grin and bear it."

"Hahako, how much longer?" asked Mamako.

"We're almost there. About one more second. Here we are!"

"What, alrea—"

But before Masato could finish, they'd arrived.

The sensation of movement changed from forward to upward. They were rising.

The cocoon of white hands opened…and they were in an entrance hall, lit by a pale blue glow.

"This…is a lot like the entrance to Catharn Castle."

"Yes—this is a castle. Deathmother Castle, the residence of Porta's mother—Saori Hotta, who now calls herself Dark-Mom Deathmother."

"Dark-Mom Deathmother? That's…certainly a choice."

"Perhaps she's trying to get in the spirit of the game world. I won't name names, but she might be similar to your mother, Wise."

"That counts as naming names! …But, like, you're totally on the money. My mom was super proud of calling herself the Queen of the Night. I thought I was gonna die from the secondhand embarrassment. Putting that aside…Hahako, what now?"

"You'll have help. First…"

But before Hahako could say anything further, a dark swirl appeared behind her.

Something like yellow caution tape shot out of it, wrapping itself around her.

"Whoa! What the—?"

"This…is a tool only those with Producer privileges can access. My actions have been severely curtailed. This will not be easy to free myself from."

"Producer privileges…then Porta's mom is doing this? Damn!"

Hahako was dragged into the dark swirl. "Oh my!" "Wait!" "Why, you!" All four of them grabbed on and tried to pull her back, but to no avail.

"Resistance is futile. Her privileges are too powerful. Resign yourselves."

"But…!"

"This is merely a movement restriction. Don't worry—I'm in no danger. Also…I fear someone has come to peek at the source of this commotion. The child you're looking for is right around the corner. See?"

"Huh? …Oh! Porta!"

Their former party member was at the end of the long hallway inside the entrance. "Whoa?!" She was wearing the black Heavenly Kings coat, and only her face was peering around a pillar. She immediately turned and fled.

"Hurry after her," Hahako suggested. "That's why I brought you here."

"Yes, that's right. Ma-kun! Girls!"

Mamako's cry gave the others the push they needed.

"...Right, let's go!"

"Thanks, Hahako! We owe you one!"

"We'll make it up to you someday!"

"No need. Oh, right... I was about to say—there are those in the Rebellion who will help you. They're not always honest about their feelings... but they're all good girls at heart. I hope you'll all become friends..."

That last bit sounded like something they'd have preferred not to hear. But with that, Hahako was pulled into the swirl. Once she was inside, it vanished.

"Help within the Rebellion? I could name a few people who seem *un*likely to ever help, but..."

"Hahako probably jumped to conclusions. The three stupid Heavenly Kings probably did something dumb and it just worked out in our favor."

"Extremely likely. I feel like attempting to contact them would just be more trouble than it's worth, so let's do our best to avoid them at all costs."

"Yep," Masato said. "Let's just go after Porta. We're in enemy territory. I know we want to do this fast but keep your guard up!"

He drew the Holy Sword Firmamento and took a firm grip on the hilt.

Wise manifested her magic tome. Her other hand was preemptively gripping a jewel that could cure magic seal. Ready for anything.

Medhi took a few practice swings with her staff. Ready for the attack. Even though she was the healer.

With everyone ready...

"Okay! Ma-kun, girls—let's clear this dungeon!"

Holding boxes of cookies in both hands, Mamako dashed ahead.

"Wait, Mom?! You can't just charge forward! Look at what you're holding?!"

"It'll be fine! I individually wrapped the cookies! They won't crumble if the boxes get a little shaken up!"

"That's not my concern! ...Argh! After her!"

An army of Skeleton Knights were attempting to block Mamako's charge.

But she didn't even slow down. She just ran right into them! "My!"

High-level undead! "Hello!" Unleashing savage attacks! "Oh, lovely!" But she just seemed pleased to see them! "You all match!" And she elegantly dodged her way past!

This was the special Mom skill, **A Mother's Parry**!

She had urgent business. But friendly neighborhood housewives were in her path!

She couldn't just ignore them. But she couldn't let herself get trapped in a long conversation!

At times like this, it was an important skill to deflect their approach and quickly move on without giving a bad impression.

"If you have a skill like that, why does it never activate when we're shopping?!"

"It's up to Mamako when to use it. Oh, right! ...*Spara la magia per mirare... Forte Vento!* And! *Forte Vento!*"

"Let's clear these enemies out of our way and get after her! Raghh!"

Wise's fierce torrent of winds lifted the Skeleton Knights off their feet, and then Medhi hit them with a sideways swing from her staff, sending them flying.

"Yes! Once they're in the air, they're mine—!"

"No, secure us a path through here."

"Okay..."

It was the perfect chance, but she was right. Masato glumly waved his sword back and forth, clearing a path between the enemies. They were soon through the Skeleton Knights as well.

They could still see Mamako ahead of them. She'd stopped in her tracks.

"Right, catch up with her! Mom! Don't get too far ahead!"

"Oh, Ma-kun! Stop! Don't come this way! You'll get stuck!"

"Huh?"

It was too late to stop. They'd already caught up with her.

It was the end of the central hallway, the entrance to the next area.

There was a huge space in front of them, like a ballroom. Gorgeous chandeliers dangled from the ceiling, and they really drew the eye...

But there were squares drawn on the ground, each about a meter across—and the one the party was standing on had the word START written on it.

"What the... Hey, we're stuck on this square! Like, there are invisible walls around it!"

"Yes…the moment I got here, I was trapped," said Mamako.

"Yikes…and we all ran headlong into that trap, huh?" asked Wise.

"Maybe so…," replied Medhi. "It looks like there's a line of squares winding around the room all the way to the exit…like a board game."

"Exactly! This is a board game of traps I made!"

Porta's voice came from the exit at the end of the hall by the square marked GOAL.

"Yo, Porta! Got a moment?"

"Wh-what is it? I'm one of the Four Heavenly Kings, so that makes us enemies now! We shouldn't be chatting!"

"Good morning!" Masato yelled, as cheerily as possible.

"…Huh?" Porta's eyes went wide, then she blinked at him.

"Ah, yeah, I guess it's not morning anymore… I just wanted to say that, though."

"Totally," Wise agreed. "If you can't greet everyone, it's like the day never started!"

"It's an important ritual that keeps the whole party together."

"Hee-hee-hee. Everyone missed your cheerful voice this morning, Porta, dear. Shall we? …One, two… Porta!"

"Morning!" "Yoohoo!" "Hello!" "Did you remember to eat breakfast?"

They spoke on top of one another, but everyone said something different.

However, the effect was the same. Tears welled up in Porta's eyes. Even so…

"Th-that makes me really happy, but it won't change anything! I have to protect my mommy! I have to fight for her!"

Porta had almost taken a step toward them, but she forced herself to stop. She turned around and ran off.

"Just hearing us say hello made her that happy… Mom, what do you make of it?" said Masato.

"She's definitely forcing herself. I had hoped she was enjoying being with her mother, but it seems that's not the case. I'm getting worried now."

"Yeah. We've gotta follow her and get her to tell us what's going on. So…"

They were already at the trap-based board game's start.

A giant die appeared in midair, falling into Masato's hands.

"Let's take on this so-called 'trap' challenge from our adorable little Porta, shall we? Here goes!"

Masato threw the die. It rolled across the floor, and the number it showed...was a 2.

Masato moved forward two spaces and saw something written on the square.

CONGRATULATIONS! YOU GET A WONDERFUL POWER-UP ITEM!

A tiny treasure chest appeared before him.

"Wow! Lucky start! ...Or maybe not..."

There was a note stuck to the chest...

This is a trap! Don't open it!

...in Porta's handwriting.

"So...I shouldn't open it...but..."

If Porta was their enemy now, would she leave a note to help him?

Maybe this note was the trap and there really was a wonderful item inside.

Masato stared at the chest.

"It's a game of traps...traps are the point. So Porta's note must be the trap, and I'm going to get an amazing treasure perfect for me! I'm sure of it!"

No adventurer could resist a treasure chest! His appetites spurred him to open it...

And the trap activated. Inside: a debuff effect that dramatically lowered his attack.

"Aughhhhhhhhhhhh! Damn iiiiiiiiiit! I-it really was a trap! And the chest is empty, too!"

"Oh my! You may have overthought that one."

"No...he got greedy, and paid the price."

"Jeez, no self-control at all. But I'm next!"

Wise's turn. She scooped up the die, and hurled it, rolling...a 2.

"Ugh! Same as Masato. Whatever...unlike Masato, I'm not activating any dumb traps. C'mon, move. These squares aren't exactly roomy."

"Argh..."

Masato had been on all fours, wracked with despair, but Wise pushed him aside. A new tiny chest appeared.

This is a trap! Don't open it!

There was another note from Porta...but the top of the chest had an illustration of a necklace called Prevenire, which could completely prevent your magic from getting sealed.

A flicker of lust crossed Wise's eyes.

"Th...th-that's...! W-wait—no, it can't be?!"

"Come on, Wise. You know it's a trap. It will always be a trap."

"I know! I know it's a trap! I'm just gonna...take a peek." *Click.*

Wise opened the lid a fraction of an inch, peering inside.

The trap activated. Inside: a debuff effect that sealed her magic.

"Arghhhhhhhhh! Damn iiiiiiiiiiiiiit!"

"And you had the gall to lecture me on self-control. I'm ashamed to be in the same party as you."

"Oh my! Wise also let herself get tricked! Too bad!"

"Masato and Wise were easily fooled by Porta's strategy. But I won't go down so easily! My self-control is a rock, unyielding in any situation!"

Medhi's turn. She rolled the die...and got a 4.

She sailed past Masato and Wise, where they lay curled up in heaps. When she reached the fourth square, words appeared.

You accidentally broke the wall! Until you clean it up, you can't roll again!

Apparently.

"I broke a wall? I have done no such thing, so this must be invalida—"

A small wall rose up right next to Medhi.

There was a list posted to it ranking the heroines. Mamako was first. Wise was second. Third was, of all people, Shiraaase. There were a *lot* of other girls' names under that...

98: Pebble (Female)

99: Medhi

100: Horse Poop (Female)

Medhi's eyes immediately clouded over, and a jet-black aura sprang up around her. She began wordlessly kicking the wall. *Thud, thud, thud!* A string of yakuza kicks.

Porta had left another note explaining, *This list was generated randomly and is not true!* But Medhi didn't notice *that.*

No self-control here. No use trying to stop her. Just leave her to it.

"Medhi's particularly fixated on results and rankings...that was already in effect, then to have her between a pebble and some horse poop...although I am curious how you determine a pebble's gender."

"That ranking might actually be totally real? I bet it is. At least, I hope is. Please."

"Poor Medhi got tricked, too! Well, then."

It was finally Mamako's turn.

"Mom, be careful! Porta's been with us a long time and knows exactly what our weaknesses are."

"I doubt she has a way to stop your domination, but…better safe than sorry."

"Yes…this is a serious contest between Porta and myself! …Hyah!"

Cradling the cookies in one hand, she rolled the die with the other… and got a 6.

When Mamako reached the square, it read…

Bargains galore! Take the transport circle directly to the store!

A direct hit to Mamako's heart!

"Oh my! A sale?! I wonder which store!" she fretted.

"Mom, calm down! It's a trap! Definitely don't go!"

"Hahako's been captured, so if you get transported somewhere, you can't come back! We don't have any clue how to get back here, so I don't think I could transport you back!"

"R-right. This is a trap! I have to stay calm and… Oh, my!"

A flyer had fluttered down in front of Mamako.

There was a note from Porta in the corner.

This is the trap's switch! Don't press it!

"Oh dear. The sale ends today! And there's a coupon attached!"

Snap.

Before she could stop herself, Mamako's hand grabbed the flyer.

A magic circle appeared at her feet. The light of the transport spell enveloped her.

"…Oh no…"

"Aughhhh! What were you *thinking*?"

"Mamako's really getting teleported out?! Masato! Do something, fast!"

"I know, but I can't leave my square! Mom, isn't there anything you can do?"

"Well…I suppose this leaves me with no choice. I know this isn't ideal, but…it is an emergency. Ma-kun!"

"What? You know a way…uh?"

Mamako had thrown something at him.

The boxes of cookies. It was close, but he managed to catch them both.

"I'll leave those with you, Ma-kun! Make sure you say hello to Porta's mother! Tell her I wish her well! Please!"

"People can't leave their squares, but inanimate objects can... No, wait, that's the last thing that matters now! Can't you use your mom powers to smash the game and evade—augh!"

Too late. With a smile and a wave, Mamako vanished...

Back in Catharn, at the Mom Shop:

"...Reports are increasing? How so?"

"Our warnings are spreading, and the pins in question are being steadily recovered...but before they know it, the children have them on again. They just find them somewhere."

Shiraaase had stopped by and was skimming reports, listening to Mone. The situation appeared grim.

"They must be infinitely spreading...like there's a sale on pins. No way to stay on top of things."

"And there's a Black Friday rush on SOSes from moms. Although some people are starting to give up, saying all children eventually grow up and leave their parents."

"That is certainly true, but when you write that in letters smudged with tears, it isn't convincing."

"Yeah. The letters themselves prove how sad and lost these mothers feel...mm? What's that?"

"Is something wrong?"

A magic circle had appeared at the front of the shop.

Light swelled up from it...and Mamako appeared.

""Huh? Mamako?!""

"...Oh, my? Is this where the sale is?"

Everyone stared at each other, blinking.

Back in Deathmother Castle, Porta's game of traps was still in progress.

A screen showed where Mamako had been sent, but it soon vanished.

"To the Mom Shop, huh? …Eh, better than an unfamiliar location. Guess we don't have to worry about her."

"On the other hand, our combat potential's taken a huge hit. This could be bad news for us…," said Wise. "Masato, you'd better not collapse in a heap of tears wailing about how you can't do anything without your mommy."

"Like hell I would! We've just gotta grit our teeth and make it through this on our own. We've all grown enough!"

"True. Right, then…"

Back to the game.

Masato's turn. The die rolled over to him like a puppy that wanted to play, and he tossed it.

He rolled a 6.

"One, two…Medhi, coming through!"

"Go right ahead… I'm almost done cleaning… Uh, wait, Masato! I don't see Mamako anywhere! What happened?!"

Medhi had finally recovered from her rage. "Wise, fill her in."

"Righty-oh." Masato left them to it, moving to his new square. The following words materialized on it:

THE FOUR HEAVENLY KINGS APPEAR! YOU CAN'T PROCEED UNLESS YOU BEAT THEM!

He hoped he was reading that wrong.

"Sheesh. Here? Now? Right into the fire, huh? Can we not?"

Just in case, Masato readied the boxes of cookies, so he could offer them up at a moment's notice. "Oh, wait, wrong thing!" He tried to switch to his weapon but failed to make it in time.

The magic circle on the floor lit up, and the Libere Rebellion's Four Heavenly Kings appeared.

Anti-Mom Amante. Scorn-Mom Sorella. Frighten-Mom Fratello.

Three powerful foes appeared inches from Masato's face!

"If I can say one thing first… You're *way* too close! Think before you spawn!"

"I thought the same thing! Also, don't scream in my face! You got spit on me!"

"Come on, Fratelloooo! You're squishing meeee! Move closer to Masatooo!"

"I-I'm a man, so…I can get real up close and personal to him and it ain't gonna bother me!"

"R-right…I'm fine with it, too. Even though I know you're really a girl. Mm."

Welp. The Heavenly Kings were here.

Wise and Medhi tried to run over but were stuck in their squares. Masato had no way of retreating. Therefore: Masato vs Three Heavenly Kings.

"We can't even move, but I've gotta fight all three of you? This is a mess. I don't suppose I can persuade you to just let me pass, since you did all help invite us here?"

"Nope. That was all Hahako jumping to conclusions. We're still enemies. So…Masato Oosuki!"

"Unh!"

A fierce battle began!

"Masatoooo! Roooock!"

"C'mon, sonny! One, two…"

"Three?"

Masato threw out rock. All three of the Heavenly Kings threw out scissors.

Masato defeated the Four Heavenly Kings!

"Yes! I win… Wait, that doesn't count! Quit screwing around!"

"No, victory is yours, Masato Oosuki. There were no specific instructions on how to determine a winner, so this is a legitimate fight, and a legitimate outcome. I shouldn't have to explain that, though! Humph."

"……Seriously?"

Was Amante telling the truth? He glanced at Sorella and Fratello, and they both nodded.

Then Masato had really won……?

"Masato, don't let them trick you! This is the game of traps!"

"And you're up against the Four Heavenly Kings! Think rationally! The slightest error could mean your life!"

"O-oh, right… You can't fool me!"

Masato braced the box of cookies… "Wait, not that!" He didn't really have anything to brace, though.

Amante just looked disgusted. "Jeez, you really can't figure it out without me explaining? Fine…Sorella. Show him the video."

"Right, riiiight…eyes to the waaaall…"

A giant magic tome appeared above her head, shining a light against the wall like a projector.

It showed footage of Porta from that morning: waking up in her luxurious bedroom, washing her face, changing... "Privacy!" "Don't watch, Masatoooo." "G-got it..." Amante and Sorella clapped their hands over his eyes during the most important part.

Then the next scenes made Masato want to cover his eyes himself.

Porta eating alone next to a row of stuffed animals.

Running to her mother's side, but not even allowed to say, "Good morning."

Announcing she'd do her best for her mother, but getting no smiles, not even a glance in her direction.

But even then, gamely smiling and dashing away. At that, the video ended.

"See, Masato Oosuki? How did that make you feel?"

"Feel? It's beyond words."

Immeasurably frustrated, he let out an agonized sigh.

"You're not gonna tell me that was a fake and this is another trap, right?"

"Sonny. I swear on the manly soul within me. Every moment of that was the God's honest truth."

"Crap...if Fratello says so, it must be true..."

"Mm. I'm a man, so I don't lie. No trickery here."

"Sooooo, you seeee..."

Sorella showed him a piece of paper.

If no results are achieved within a minute, everyone will be sent back to the start!

Everything Porta wrote was definitely true. No lies there.

"...Amante, explain."

"Our Master is Porta's mom. But she's a mom who treats her kid like that. So she's our enemy. And the way she treats us...just remembering it makes my blood boil. Rrgh!"

"Wh-what? What happened?"

"Never mind. Point is, the Master needs to be eliminated. But Porta won't agree to that."

"Of course not...she loves her mom."

"I have no idea why. Anyway, we tried to talk her into it, but just made her angry...so she locked us in here. If we don't obey the rules, we can't leave this dumb game."

"So you picked rock, paper, scissors so we could settle things fast. I see...yeah, no way I'd figure *that* out without an explanation."

"Fair enough... But now that you get it, enough talking."

All three of them turned on their heels.

"Oh, Masatoooo...if you don't miiiind..."

"I'm certainly angry, too. But I can't agree to fight Porta's mom. I'm glad you told me what's going on with her, though."

"Mm. I thought you'd say that, sonny. In the end, we'll always be enemies."

"We're going to defeat the Master like the enemy she is. You and your party have fun with this game. See you later."

The three of them tried to walk away...

""""Mmphah!"""" *Thud!*

...but couldn't. There were invisible walls around the squares.

Having slammed face-first into them, all three turned around, teary-eyed and red-nosed.

"You really can't get it together, huh?"

"Sh-shut up! It, uh, seems we have to clear the board game before we can leave... Masato Oosuki! Hand me the die!"

"Who's got it now?"

"It's my turn, so it's with me! Here goes!" Wise was after Masato. She rolled a 6. "Argh!"

And the die went to Medhi.

"Anything but a 4. Please not a 4."

Medhi rolled a 4. "Erk...?!"

So...

"Wise, please squeeze in closer." *Push.*

"I can't! Masato! You scoot over!" *Flat.*

"Impossible! Stop pushing! Augh, look, we're crushing Fratello!"

"I got no issues being pressed up against you, sonny! No skin off my nose!" *Flat.*

"Tough luck, Masatooo. You're stuck between the two flat giiiirls." *Squish.*

"Sorella! Stop talking crap and gimme the die! Now!"

"Whaaat? Aren't I neeext?" *Squeeze?*

"No, I am! If I don't roll now, I'm gonna suffocate between your boobs...wait...was that your plan all along—?!""""

There they were, on the eighth square of the game of traps.

Who would be the first to break free? This was the start of a fierce battle between six—"...Gah..." "Amante's ooout!"—*five* people crammed into a single square meter.

Now, in the throne room.

"If they somehow cooperated with one another, that would be my ideal outcome, but...it seems unlikely."

Dark-Mom Deathmother was watching the commotion through a crystal ball, her expression softening...

But only momentarily. Her face quickly stiffened, and she looked away.

"...You've escaped your bonds already? Impressive."

"It was extremely difficult. Your resolve is not easily overcome."

The floor beside the throne swelled up and transformed into Hahako.

And yet Hahako smiled at Dark-Mom Deathmother, displaying no objection to her treatment.

"...What?"

"You don't hate children, do you?"

"No. I have no reason to. I don't think of them as any kind of evil."

"You don't hate your own child, either."

Dark-Mom Deathmother did not have an answer to that.

Instead, she waved at hand at the crystal ball, changing what it displayed.

Porta was dashing around the castle, placing stuffed animals in every corner.

Dark-Mom Deathmother watched closely.

Hahako's smile grew even happier.

"You *are* a mother."

"Stop. That point I must refute."

"Oh? Why?"

"Liking children makes one a mother? That's not how it works, is it? By that logic, you could become a mother regardless of blood ties, gender, or age. That's just wrong."

"Oh my. You certainly are particular. Then...do you demand such precise responses from children as well?"

"No. I demand nothing at all. I have no intention of raising them strictly to my own specifications."

"Very well. Then I'm at a loss. You fit no type of mother I'm aware of... and I've gathered data on all the mothers participating in this game."

"Of course. A mother like me would never consider participating in a game that required a mother's presence."

"What...?"

Dark-Mom Deathmother dismissed the image of Porta and rose from her throne.

"Adventuring with one's mother is absurd. The world inside the game ought to be for the children alone. A mother's participation is unnecessary."

"I disagree. Adventuring with your mother is a wonderful thing."

"But doing so stymies the child's growth."

"It does?"

"Does a child learn everything in life at their mother's side? That's clearly not true."

"Well...no, but..."

"Children form relationships with each other, experience things together, and learn much in the process. Hahako, listen closely."

Dark-Mom Deathmother turned to face Hahako.

"Children grow up even if they *have no mothers*."

This was Dark-Mom Deathmother's core belief.

At the very least, in this moment, her faith in it was absolute.

"Hahako, if you wish to make those three your children, go right ahead. I grant you permission. Is that your desire?"

"I-it is, but..."

"But consider whether they really need you as a mother. Consider if that really is in their best interests. If you make the wrong choice, it will be painful for all of you."

Seeing the troubled look on Hahako's face, Dark-Mom Death-mother patted her on the shoulder.

And then she headed for the private quarters behind the throne.

"...Could I ask one last thing?" said Hahako.

"Depends on the question."

"It seems like you are treating your own daughter harshly, trying to turn her against you. It seems you welcome the children seeing you as a nemesis and coming here to defeat you. What is it you're planning? What are you thinking?"

Dark-Mom Deathmother paused.

"Everything I do is for the children. Everything and anything."

She spoke softly, as if affirming each and every word. Then she stepped through the door.

All alone, Hahako was left trapped in her thoughts.

"Children grow up even if they have no mothers...then perhaps it is better if I don't become a mother. Am I not needed...?"

This was starting to sound true. Hahako grew despondent...

Hahako was a being who wished to become a mother.

The strength of that feeling allowed her to use mom power every bit as powerful as the ultimate mother, Mamako.

Mom power had three main sources: the mother herself, Mother Earth, and Mother Ocean. Hahako was not yet a mother herself, so her power was drawn from a close connection to the earth and the ocean.

Which was why this was happening.

A dreadnought warship flying a Catharn flag was patrolling the vast expanse of ocean.

"Mm...? The waves...stopped?"

A sailor peered over the prow, unable to believe his eyes.

The water's gentle lapping had ceased completely.

This wasn't a "calm." The wind was still blowing. The ship's sails were swollen with it, and the ship itself was progressing at a steady speed—only the motion of the water itself had ceased.

Then...

"Wh-what the—?!" screamed another sailor—this one was posted in the crow's nest at the top of the sail.

"What's wrong? Report!"

"There's a depression in the sea straight ahead! Distance...crap! The depression's getting bigger by the second. I can't measure the distance! We gotta turn now or the ship will fall in!"

"Got it! Hard to starboard! Emergency maneuvers! All hands, grab on to something! Don't fall overboard!"

The helmsman spun the wheel and the ship listed dangerously to the right, turning as tightly as it could.

The massive depression in the water was closing in fast, big enough to swallow an entire town. The ship skirted the edges of it—and pulled away.

With that narrow escape behind them, the ship remained on high alert. The depression had stopped expanding, so they began sailing around it.

"Looks like it's over... Oh! Is Her Majesty the Queen all right? Go check on her!"

"I'm fine. It certainly was quite a lurch and took me by surprise, but as you can see, I escaped unscathed."

"Y-your Majesty...! Oh..."

Queen of Catharn (the queen of Catharn) stepped out of the ship's cabin.

Even on deck, she wore a magnificent dress...but appeared to have been dining when the ship turned. The queen had a fork, a knife, and boiled lobster stuck in the curls of her hair.

"Not entirely unscathed, I see... My humblest apologies."

"Don't be ridiculous. I am perfectly unharmed. I would, however, appreciate an explanation."

"R-right...you see..."

Unable to tear his eyes away from the lobster on her head—*c'mon, get it together, don't look*—the sailor explained the situation.

Queen of Catharn stared at the depression, deep in thought.

"I did not imagine it being this dire... I was right to verify matters in person. We need to take drastic action. Let's head back to the Catharn capital, please."

"Aye-aye, Your Majesty!"

He saluted the lobs—no, the queen—and ran off down the deck.

"Friction between parents and children the world over. Disturbances in Mother Earth and Mother Ocean. I imagine these phenomena are related somehow...which means the only one who can resolve this is..."

The queen closed her eyes, and despite the urgency of the situation... smiled.

Mom Roster Profile 2

Kazuno

■Age:
Younger than Medhimama, older than Shirase.

■Hobbies:
Hosts, of course... Cough, cough, I mean, art appreciation!

■Specialties:
I can accurately identify how muscular someone is no matter what they're wearing. Only works on men, though.

■Best Feature:
My slammin' body. Every feature is my best feature. ...Granted, I'm using a transformation spell, but let's not fuss about the details.

■Childhood Dream:
Even as a kid, all I dreamed about was becoming filthy rich.

■Catchphrase:
"Genya." I just enter the club and the number one host, Genya, sits down right next to me... Huh? That's not what you meant by 'catch'?

■Child-Rearing Philosophy:
My parents let me do as I pleased, so I let her do the same.

■To Your Beloved Child:
I'm not sure what to put here... Ummm... I've got nothing in particular to say. If you're doing well, that's good. I'm out here doing my own thing.
    ...You could call me sometimes, you know.
    Later, you dumb daughter.

Chapter 3 Meetings, Partings, and Reunions. The Bonds We Share...Really Rattle Us.

Back at Porta's game of traps at Deathmother Castle.

As the game progressed, certain feelings were blossoming between Masato and the Heavenly Kings.

They were staring passionately into each other's eyes.

"Masato Oosuki. I just all of a sudden can't take my eyes off you... Are these emotions welling up with in me...? No, don't make me explain. Humph."

"Amante...thank you. You're making me blush."

"Aaaactually...I'm also starting to think you're pretty coooool. Are you at all into older womeeen? I could really teach you a thing or twoooo. Mwa-ha-haaa."

"Sorella, that sultry look in your eyes is...definitely tempting..."

"Sonny, you already know how I feel. I been fond of ya since we met, and I'd love nothin' better than to stay by your side. You in?"

"Fratello, you're speaking your truth, and that makes me so happy. Like, I'm all choked up."

Masato and the three girls stared at one another, hands on their hearts, feeling the beating within.

Ba-bump. Ba-bump. Ba-bump. Their hearts pounded away.

"Amante, Sorella, Fratello...thank you all. I know..."

""""We'll always be together!""""

"Always... Yeah, like hell we will! Knock it off already! Pleeeeeeeease, you stupid die!! Stop being an asshole!"

Masato's turn. He hurled the die...

...and rolled a 1.

""""Aughhhhhhhhhhhhhh?!""""

"Hell yeah!"

He stepped right over the words YOU CAN'T REACH THE GOAL UNTIL YOU ROLL A 1! and leaped onto the final square.

Masato cleared the game of traps!

Wise and Medhi had cleared it earlier and were napping in the hall with the boxes of cookies. Their eyes fluttered open.

"......Mm? Is it finally over? That took *way* too long. Seriously, are you cursed or something?"

"I kept count for the first twenty tries, but...what was the final number?"

"Fifty-eight! I went so far beyond anger, I achieved enlightenment!"

"Missing a one in six chance to that degree is downright miraculous," marveled Wise. "I'm impressed!"

"Anyway," said Medhi, "all three of us cleared the game, which means..."

"Exactly!"

Masato, Wise, and Medhi turned and smiled.

The three Heavenly Kings were permanently stuck one step from the exit and glared at them more balefully than any vengeful spirit. Veins throbbing.

"This isn't funny! The happier you look, the angrier I get!"

"Arghhh... Unbelieeeevable! We were getting to know each other soooo well, only for you to betray us like thiiiis! Scuuum!"

"Don't blame us," said Wise. "You just didn't get lucky."

"Probably karma coming back to bite you," said Medhi.

"Say, sonny, I don't suppose you could somehow pull me out with you...?"

"Afraid not, Fratello. We're enemies, after all. We can't support your schemes. Sorry."

They turned to leave.

"Masato Oosuki! Just so we know, what's your goal here?"

"Our goal? First...Porta. We need to find her, and talk."

"Then we'll leave her to youuuu. She's soooooo stubborn! We don't stand a chaaaance. Buuut..."

"We'll take care of Porta's mother, too. We're not letting you go after her."

"'Fraid that's where we draw the line. We'll be outta this game soon enough."

"And then we'll show up at the perfect moooooment! And get herrrr! Mwah-ha-haaah!"

"And if you try and stop us, we'll take you down with her. Be ready to get kicked out of the way!"

"You're hell bent on attacking her mother, huh? Jeez."

Masato glanced at the three of them, and grinned.

"Wh-what?"

"No big deal. Just…in that video you showed us, all three of you were trying to cheer Porta up. And defending her."

"Well, suuuure… We can't agree with her desire to have a moooom… but she's so earneeest. I meeean…"

"As a man, I have a strong sense of duty. Something touches my heart, I'm gonna take action."

"Huh… I guess Hahako was right. Deep down, you aren't bad people. Maybe given the right opportunity, you'll all change."

"Don't be ridiculous. Are you legitimately stupid? Idiot," Amante snapped.

"Yeah, just an idiot talking to himself. Forget I said anything." Masato grinned, deflecting it easily.

Masato, Wise, and Medhi glanced at each other, nodded gravely, and ran off, following the trail of stuffed animals in the halls to resume their pursuit of Porta.

Meanwhile, at the Mom Shop in Catharn…

Mamako, Mone, and Shiraaase were gathered around the table, frowning at a map of the world.

"Well, Mamako? Think you can pull off the transport?" asked Mone.

"Mm…I'm not so sure. I've never used a spell like that and have no idea how it feels. And I don't even know where the place is…"

Mamako was holding a jewel that served as a transport item. She was trying to send herself back to Deathmother Castle, but without much success.

"Then perhaps you should ask Mother Earth for help? That might work somehow," suggested Shiraaase.

"Yes…I suppose I should."

She put the map of the world on the ground, hoping it would help.

Then she held the Holy Sword of Mother Earth, Terra di Madre, aloft.

"Mother Earth…I want to hurry back to my beloved son and his friends…if you know how that feels, lend me your power!"

The note answered her call, showing their location on the map—the special child-locating mom skill, A Mother's Fangs…

…did nothing. Total silence.

"Oh my! It seems I've failed."

"Usually, no matter how insane it sounds, you can easily pull it off…but if this won't work, your opponent clearly has countermeasures in place."

"I wonder what kind of countermeasures?" said Mone. "Hmm… maybe, like, a barrier around the place they're at? So you can't locate it?"

"That could be… It does feel a bit like that," said Mamako. "But… hmm…" She cocked her head, staring at her feet. "It's like the earth isn't feeling well…and doesn't really approve of me finding Ma-kun and running to him."

"It doesn't approve? You mean, it doesn't think you need to go?" asked Shiraaase.

"Like it wants you to let them handle it?" said Mone.

"Yes…maybe that's it…"

Mamako sheathed her sword, and slowly sat down.

"I can let Ma-kun and the girls handle the rest… That much I feel is true. I mean, they've all grown so strong. Both in battle and their everyday lives. Even without me at their side and helping, I'm sure they can take care of themselves."

"R-really? I guess I wouldn't know," Mone said.

"They certainly have become much more reliable, but…"

"I know! So…as worried as I am, part of me thinks…maybe this is for the best."

As children grow, they stop needing your help. A parent's role comes to an end.

That's a joyous thing, but also…very sad.

Dealing with emotions all parents eventually experience, Mamako smiled weakly and stared out the window.

Mone and Shiraaase glanced at each other, worried.

"Personally, I want to have my mother spoil me all the time, and I never want to leave her side so…"

"Yes, Mone, you were created to be a Dark God of Spoiling, so you would think that way. You may be working at the Mom Shop to overcome that need and be more independent, but changing what lies deep down is not so easily done."

"Blegh, you make it sound like I haven't grown at all! That's not fair."

"No, no, I didn't mean that…but, well, generally speaking, I think Mamako is right. As children grow up, they become independent, and parents have to let them… Oh…!"

"Mm? Ms. Shiraaase, what is it?"

Shiraaase had jumped to her feet and run over to the counter.

She picked up the documents on the children's rapid growth, thinking quickly.

"Children growing...they no longer need parents...mothers wrestling with those emotions, but pulling back...mom power responds, reducing its output...this is bad news."

"Oh? How so?"

"That means everything is working out exactly as our enemy planned."

Her methods may be forceful, but children growing up and leaving their parents was a natural process

Using that natural process to make mothers step back from the spotlight of their own volition...would mean the Libere Rebellion's goal of eliminating mothers would easily come to pass.

I can't just let her have things her way...but...

Mamako was their most effective measure against this sort of thing, but she was on the verge of deciding it was best to step back.

And even the powers that mothers drew upon were giving up.

What should I do?

How did one overcome a disadvantage created by a logically sound argument? Shiraaase had to think of something...

As she tried...

They heard a horse whinny. A carriage had pulled up in front of the Mom Shop.

A castle dignitary came rushing in, in full formal attire.

"I apologize for the sudden intrusion! Forgive me, but the situation is dire! Is Mamako Oosuki's party here?"

"Ah, yes, I am, at least..."

"Oh! So you are! I see the children aren't with you but...p-please, come to the castle posthaste! The queen has an urgent request for you!"

"The queen? Oh, my! What could it be?"

Mamako, Shiraaase, and Mone looked at one another, baffled.

Since there was no telling when more concerned mothers would arrive with reports of rapid child maturation, they couldn't very well leave the Mom Shop unattended—so Mone remained behind.

Mamako and Shiraaase accepted the invitation to the castle. The carriage swept them along at top speed.

Once they'd arrived, they were invited not to a reception room, but to the queen's private quarters, as friends.

"Your Majesty, pardon the intrusion."

"Oh my! Mamako! Thank you for coming. And you must be... Ms. Shiraaase, from management, right? I believe we met at the prince's courtship ball."

"I'm honored you remembered me. It is likewise an honor to meet Your Majesty in—in?"

Mid formal greeting, Shiraaase froze—her eyes glued to the knife, fork, and lobster lodged in the queen's hairdo.

"Is this a test of my comedic timing?"

"Er, um...I doubt that very much..."

"Whatever is the matter? Is there something on my head? ...Oh, right! I've just returned from a scouting mission and haven't had time to freshen up. I must be rather disheveled! How embarrassing... Ladies?"

The door to the side room opened, and several ladies-in-waiting filed in.

They pretended to redo her hair, while surreptitiously removing the cutlery and lobster, then left—all without a trace of surprise ever crossing their faces. "Much better. A relief, yes?" "Yes." "Absolutely." Mamako and Shiraaase were much more relieved than the queen herself.

Anyway. They were led to a nearby couch, and the queen sat down opposite them.

"First, from the bottom of my heart, thank you for responding to my invitation on such short notice. I cannot thank you enough. However, I don't see your children anywhere...?"

"Ma-kun and the girls...they're, um, on an adventure..."

"An adventure? They went without you?"

"Not quite, no... How should I put this..."

"Mamako's party was in the midst of solving one incident when an enemy scheme resulted in Mamako being sent back to Catharn."

"Oh my! How awful."

The queen gave Mamako a long, searching look. She seemed concerned about Mamako's very un-Mamako-like hemming and hawing.

"It sounds as if you're very busy—I do hope my summons isn't inter-rupting anything."

"N-no, don't worry about that. I believe we can leave that matter in the children's hands. Even without me by their side, they will undoubt-edly solve everything themselves. I am so proud of them, you know."

Mamako smiled. She seemed to think this was a bright, cheery smile.

It did not look like one to the queen's eyes. Her frown deepened.

"Ms. Shiraaase, do you know what's happened to Mamako? She seems gloomy...almost *depressed*."

"I can infooorm you that your assessment is entirely correct."

Shiraaase showed the queen a number of reports she'd brought with her from the Mom Shop.

The particular reports she'd selected were ones documenting not only the rapid growth of the children, but also the harrowing admissions from mothers who had started to accept their children's independence.

The queen soon caught on and let out a deep sigh.

"That would explain it. Well, perhaps this is actually the perfect tim-ing, then."

"Meaning?"

"Mamako has shown me how a mother should be and saved both me and my child. I owe her a great debt. I believe this is my chance to communicate something critical to her—something every mother needs to know."

"Very well. I shall leave this in Your Majesty's hands."

"Please do."

Shiraaase bowed her head with a smile.

The queen turned to face Mamako.

"Let's get down to business," she said. "Listen closely. Currently events are unfolding all over the world that may very well threaten its very existence. The situation is extremely grave."

"What? What's happening?"

"First, the earth and the sea are developing sudden depressions. I myself witnessed the development of one in the ocean's surface not long ago. Similar phenomena have been reported on land, and when these happen in populated areas, the damage is immense."

"I have seen this phenomenon myself," said Shiraaase. "A relatively small depression, roughly three meters in diameter, appeared in the middle of the Catharn capital. I nearly fell in. Twice."

"Oh dear..."

"And we cannot ignore these sad reports of unnatural child development tearing families apart. The goal of this world is for parents and children to remain close forever, to live happy lives, hand in hand. That is the ultimate theme of the world, and should that be denied, the world itself would lose its reason to exist."

"Oh my! If that happens...what will become of it...?"

"In plain terms, the game world will fail. Management will inform—no, infooorm—everyone that service is ending. Right, Ms. Shiraaase?"

"It is an honor to have you humor my peccadilloes."

Shiraaase bowed her head. It seemed they shared a love of bad puns. But this was a serious conversation.

"I believe these two phenomena are connected. Seeing you like this, Mamako, only confirms that."

"Me? Like this...?"

"Mamako, the fact that your son has grown and is pulling away from you has left you feeling lonely and depressed. *Depressed*—like the depressions forming on the earth and ocean."

"...Huh?" Mamako looked surprised.

The queen nodded. "Mother Earth and Mother Ocean grant power in response to a mother's emotions. Yet they also sense the emotions of mothers and are influenced by them. Ms. Shiraaase, this is pure speculation on my part but...from an Admin standpoint, what is your take on the matter?"

"I'm afraid I'm not that well-versed in the particulars of the game's design. No, that's not entirely true... Regardless of the design specifications, we have one individual bringing about all manner of extreme feats in the name of mothers everywhere. Someone right here with us."

"Ho-ho-ho! Indubitably. I personally saw her use a simple push on the back to break the laws between dimensions! I couldn't believe my eyes."

"This individual even influenced the game's main systems to create Hahako—just one example of the world moving in ways it was never intended to. And that daily connection to Mothers Earth and Ocean, to that incredible power—if she has shared that, consciously or not..."

"Then other mothers receive those blessings, share their feelings, and affect the earth and ocean. It seems highly plausible…if no less mind-boggling."

"Certainly. *Mind-boggling* is the perfect word."

"Um…so who are we talking about again?" asked Mamako.

The individual in question was staring blankly at Shiraaase and the queen. Total lack of self-awareness.

Regardless:

"Well, with that understood, the path is clear," said the queen. "Only one thing for us to do. Right, Mamako?"

"Er…um…"

"Let me make this simple. The two phenomena we're dealing with are connected. The earth and ocean's depressions stem from depressed mothers. The mothers are depressed because of what the Libere Rebellion is doing. Which means…"

"Which means… Oh, I see! If we can persuade Porta's mother, the Rebellion leader, then that will put an end to everything!"

"You've already identified the enemy leader? In that case…"

"Yes! Let us hear a Mamako-like response!"

"Very well! Then…"

Mamako sprang to her feet, raising her fist in the air.

Then an idea struck her, and she lowered her arm.

"…I'm sure Ma-kun and the girls will handle that. I'm better off making a nice meal and waiting for them to come back. Yes, I think that's best."

She sat down again listlessly.

But…

"That, too, is a motherly response. But Mamako—it isn't how *you* do things."

The queen caught her gaze and held it.

"Listen, Mamako. Because you lent us your power, my son, the prince, found his perfect match. They successfully married and are living happily ever after. But as a result…I grew depressed."

"What? Why…?"

"We are royals, so family matters work differently than many—but my son now has a family of his own. They have started their own lives together. That means I can no longer expect him to remain at his mother's side—especially if I have faith in him."

"That *is* true… There are times when you know it's better for your children to pull away."

"Yes. So I had to allow him his independence. And I missed him terribly. But then a thought struck me."

"…What thought?"

"I hit upon the perfect method. I can maintain a certain distance from him, yet still see his face, hear his voice, and spend as much time with him as before."

"Wh-what is this miraculous method?"

Mamako leaned in, eager to hear more. The queen smiled proudly.

"I go see him all the time."

Mamako's jaw dropped. It took a moment for the meaning to sink in. Shiraaase got there first, clapping her hands once in recognition.

The queen's grin broadened.

"It's quite simple. Anytime I have any business to take care of, we meet, talk, and spend time together. That's all! But this next part is key. Critically important. Listen carefully."

"Y-yes…go on."

"Things don't always work out that way. When I don't actually have business to take care of, I just…make some up."

"…Huh?"

"This is a trick only a mother can pull off. I think it's safe to call it a mom skill."

Imagine a mother who had just folded some laundry. By delivering it personally to a child's room, she can catch a glimpse of what her child is up to.

Imagine a child has moved into an apartment of their own, and their mother is on a sightseeing tour in the area, but she takes a break to pop in for a quick visit.

This kind of mom action is an effect of the special mom skill, A Mother's Visit. Must be.

"I mean, I want to see my son! I want to see his face, talk to him, spend time with him. And the only way to make that happen is to invent a pretext to see him! Yes…like if I were you right now, Mamako…"

"You could follow a different path from Masato's party, pursing a different goal, but the result of it—you coincidentally meet up. Or is that pushing it?"

"Oh my, Ms. Shiraaase! That *might* be pushing your luck, ho-ho-ho."

"It will likely have a huge effect on everyone she gets involved with and the world itself! How terrifyingly convenient. Heh-heh-heh."

Shiraaase and the queen shared a vaguely sinister laugh. Meanwhile, Mamako was thinking this over, taking it very seriously.

"Mamako," the queen said. "I think sometimes mothers should be a little foolish. You shouldn't pretend to be wise and hide how you feel. You shouldn't decide something is in the child's best interests. It's important to be honest with yourself as a mother. See?"

"......Yes. I *am* a mother."

Mamako slowly raised her head. No trace of doubt remained in her mind.

The queen nodded.

"Looks like we have nothing to worry about."

"No, Your Majesty. I'm sorry to make you worry. I'm fine now. I just remembered some business I have to take care of, so if you'll excuse me..."

"Ho-ho-ho! Far be it from me to get between you and your business. As the queen, I shall see the hero's mother off on her journey... Ah, right. One more thing I should mention..."

"Oh? What's that?"

"Even for you, Mamako, adventuring alone is far too dangerous. You should gather a party at the guild and prepare for the upcoming journey—this is the core principle of any RPG."

The queen gave her a wink loaded with significance.

"First, gather a party at the Adventurers Guild. I did that with Ma-kun when we first started this game! I remember it so well."

"Your show of strength caused considerable damage to the building and myself, but...good times. Let's head there again."

Mamako and Shiraaase had left the castle and were headed toward the guild, dodging depressions in the road.

There were a number of adventurers assembled outside the building.

"...Hey, look!" "What? Seriously?!" The moment they spied Mamako, a stir ran through the crowd, looks of admiration turning toward her.

"Oh my! We've already found some adventurers!"

"Hold your horses. This is the start point for all adventures in Catharn. In other words, adventurers registered here all have their levels set quite low, so they can easily join the parties of new players."

"I see! That does make sense. I feel sorry for the adventurers here, but they don't seem like they'd be very helpful."

"That is a problem... We're about to head directly to the headquarters of the enemy. Taking beginners along would just slow us down."

"Oh dear. We don't want that."

"I fear you operating on your own would get you to Masato faster than that partying with them...which means the queen's suggestion must have some other merit."

At this point, they'd reached the guild doors and stepped inside.

"Oh, there she is!"

"I'm glad she arrived before I was forced to order a second cup of tea."

Two women were resting on a couch nearby.

One wore a flashy evening gown covered in sequins. She had a deep tan and sported a pair of devil-like horns.

The other wore holy robes lavishly decorated in nouveau riche chic. She had a haughty expression on her face.

At the sight of them, Shiraaase's eyes widened, and Mamako let out a cry of surprise.

"Kazuno?! And Medhimama?!"

"Mamako, Shiraaase, 'sup? We meet again. But you're so late! I was about to *die* of boredom."

"That's a lie. You've been having a grand old time sitting here gossiping about the adventurers' muscles. I was ashamed to be seen with you."

"Spare me the kink shaming. It's none of your business what I like."

They seemed to have broken the ice, at least...

The two women rose from their seats and stepped forward.

Wise's mother, the Queen of the Night—Kazuno.

Medhi's mother, Medhimama.

There was no mistaking them.

"It really is you! I can't believe it," Mamako said.

"I agree. I never imagined you were still alive..."

"Hey! Shiraaase! What the heck? Why would you assume I died?"

"Don't pay that woman the slightest attention. She is a stealth goofball."

"Hee-hee-hee, I see! You both became close to your children, cleared the game successfully, and returned to the real world ahead of us, right? So what brings you here?"

Kazuno and Medhimama glanced at each other, and grimaced.

"Where to begin...? You know, you're better at this sort of thing, Memama. Take it away."

"I will never willingly allow you to call me that, but very well. You see..."

Medhimama took a deep breath. Ready, set...

"Kazuno and I were hired to capture the producer who fled into the game world. As for why we had been chosen, we were told the primary reason is that we have experience living in this world, but in truth, I assume the fact that we owe management was a big part of it. Neither of us was in a position to refuse, in other words. I'm afraid Kazuno and I were already acquainted with one another, having met several times during the investigations into the trouble we each caused. We contacted each other and met up here in the game world approximately one hour ago. Just as we were about to launch our investigation, we received a message from management telling us to remain on standby at the Adventurers Guild and rendezvous with Mamako. Which brings us here."

"That's the gist of it, yeah."

A hurricane of words, yet so easily understood. "Oh, I see." "Ah, yes, indeed." Mamako and Shiraaase nodded, feeling up to speed.

"That's the official version anyway. Kazuno will explain our actual motivations. Take it away."

"Er, why? Who cares...?"

"Now, now. You want to show how you've improved as a mother, don't you? Don't let shame get in your way."

"Y-you're really making me do this...ugh..."

Medhimama gave Kazuno a push, placing her in front.

Mamako and Shiraaase watched expectantly. Kazuno's gaze darted this way and that, but she finally opened her mouth.

"Well, um...I guess...I'm more of a mother than I realized, so I started thinking..."

"Thinking what?"

"'What's she up to now? Like, is she doing all right?' You know."

"Hmm...and who are you referring to?"

"Well, obviously…that dumb daughter of mine."

"G-g-good Lord! What brought this about?! Kazuno?! The woman who called herself the Queen of the Night collected hunks from towns and villages and sprawled proudly back on a chair made from hotties?! And now you're acting like a real mother and actually concerned about your daughter's well-being?!"

"Sh-Shiraaase! Don't go digging that stuff up *now!*"

"Kazuno, calm down. She's messing with you again. That's what Shiraaase does."

Even up against veteran mothers, Shiraaase was merciless. "I've discovered a rich new vein to mine." "Perhaps you should rein it in a bit…" But even with Mamako's warning, Shiraaase would continue to charge forward! Undaunted!

Kazuno appeared ready to die of humiliation, but then she suddenly smiled.

"Since my dumb daughter isn't here, I can admit it—I thought this job would be the perfect excuse to check in on her. That's why I accepted it."

Medhimama nodded in agreement.

"We heard you talking as you entered. You're headed to the enemy headquarters to meet up with the children? What's going on?"

"That's right! We have urgent business there! And while we're at it, we expect to bump into Ma-kun and the girls. That's why I need to gather a party!"

"I see. In that case…"

"We have every reason to help."

Both mothers nodded.

Kazuno produced an extravagantly decorated magic tome and gave everyone a bewitching smile.

"I can use any spell in this world with a single word. As a Great Sage…as the Queen of the Night, nay, the Night Queen, will you allow me to join your journey?"

Medhimama produced a staff studded with jewels and struck a dignified pose.

"A single swing of my new staff can protect and heal anything. Will you accept the Cleric Medhimama into your party?"

Both had top-class gear, and the ridiculous powers granted only to mothers. No party members could be better.

Mamako had no reason to turn them down. She nodded, fighting to hold back the tears.

"Kazuno, Medhimama, I'll be counting on you both."

"Thank you."

"Uh, wait, Mamako…I changed my name when I reregistered, but…oh, never mind."

Mamako held out her hand, and Medhimama and Kazuno placed theirs on it.

"Ms. Shiraaase, won't you join us?"

"If I won't get in the way, I'd be glad to. I can provide support…and lead the pep squad."

"I feel like you might just rob us of pep instead…"

"But the more the merrier!"

With Shiraaase's hand on theirs, the four mothers' hearts were one!

"It's the dawn of a Mom RPG! Let's get going."

"So I can meet all the hot slim-yet-ripped men! I'm kidding, of course."

"To complete the errand we've taken on, and while we're at it…"

"Run into our beloved children! Yay!"

The opening fanfare echoed through all four hearts, and the mothers' adventure began!

There was only one problem.

"So, what do we actually *do*? We haven't actually settled on anything." Mamako smiled.

""Er…we thought *you* had a plan.""

"Let's begin by touring the world and dealing with problems occurring in each part of it. As we resolve those issues, we can gather clues, drawing us ever closer to the truth—and the enemy boss. Probably."

"Probably…I know that's how games always work, but are we sure about this? It sounds like a lot of work, you know."

"Don't worry. No matter what trouble lies in our path, we can overcome it! With such unparalleled mothers assembled, I'm sure of it! We're a match for any challenge!"

Medhimama was really emphasizing that notion.

But then a carriage pulled up outside the guild. "Oh? It's that gentleman from earlier." The same official who'd come calling at the Mom Shop.

"Pardon me! Is Mamako Oosuki… Ah, there you are! Is this your party?"

"It is. What brings you here?"

"The queen has sent a gift! One she hopes will assist you in your adventure. Please accept it!"

Four servants came staggering in with a giant treasure chest.

At once, the chest opened! A blinding light came from within, illuminating the four expectant faces!

"Always pleased to receive financial sup—augh!" *Shock!*

"Er...y-you're kidding, right...?" *...Tremble, shudder...*

"Oh-ho? Didn't expect this!" *Grin.*

"Oh my! How lovely!" *Beam.*

There came a variety of reactions, but what lay within the chest...?!

"...This...is a trap, huh?"

Masato was sitting in front of a stuffed lizard they'd found lying on the side of a corridor.

He'd lost track of how many stuffed animals this was.

We figured if we followed the plushies, we'd find Porta, but...

...That belief had just led to their racing around the maze of Deathmother Castle corridors ever since they'd escaped the board game.

Bears, rabbits, cats, dogs...all kinds of stuffed animals, placed like they were marking the path...

But the end results?

No signs of Porta, no locations arrived at—and they were worn out from all that running.

"I can't... I'm exhausted... She's nowhere to be found..."

"And this *is* the enemy base, so the monsters here are pretty tough..."

Wise and Medhi were both collapsed against the wall—and that wall was the only thing keeping them even vaguely upright. They clearly weren't moving for a while.

So they'd been forced to take a break. Masato had sat down, too, making sure not to crush the boxes of cookies.

"Looks like she really doesn't want us getting to her mother..."

"Porta's intentions are crystal clear. Definitely a 'whatever it takes' approach..."

"Yet the way she's still looking after us is really cute."

Medhi forced herself to her feet, moving over to the lizard.

When she moved it aside, she found several HP and MP Potions behind it.

"She loves her mother. But she clearly still cares about us, too. Isn't she wonderful?"

"Yeah... But that just makes me worry more," said Masato. "As tired as we are, Porta must be running herself ragged."

"And you know she doesn't *really* want to be doing this," added Wise.

"But it's for her beloved mommy, so..."

"She's ignoring how she really feels, forcing herself to do it."

"And that'll lead to darkness growing within. Like it used to inside Medhi."

Could this be the sudden emergence of Dark Porta, throwing poison items at her friends with an adorable smile?!

"Holy crap! If Porta winds up like Medhi, it'll be the end of everything!"

"Masato? What exactly is that supposed to mean? I haven't ended anything." Medhi's smile was not a smile, and she was grinding an HP recovery potion bottle into his stomach. "Sorry, please stop." "No." She was pushing him toward the vomit threshold.

But anyway, that was enough joking around.

Masato stood up and chugged the HP potion.

"Right, let's get back to it. We've gotta catch Porta...but..."

""But...?""

But how?

Masato couldn't think of a follow-up.

...*What* should *we do?*

He had to organize his thoughts. What did they *want* to do?

Get Porta back in their party. Especially now that she'd joined the enemy side.

But Porta's mother was part of said enemy.

To get Porta back, they would have to tear apart that family bond.

"Masato?"

"Masato?"

"W-wait, I'm thinking. Um..."

They were leaning in close, their eyes demanding that he say something now. That he prove his leadership skills. "Masato?" "Masatooo?" "Wait!" Their faces were *really* close.

Focus. Think.

If they just wanted to be together, that would be one thing, but...

Porta's mother was the Rebellion leader. Mastermind of all the cases they'd resolved. The root of all evil.

And her treatment of her own daughter could hardly be called warm and doting.

That was two major problems.

We've got to do something about her mother, but…

Porta was standing in their way, trying to prevent them from reaching her. Which meant they had to talk her into stopping.

So they had to talk to Porta.

But how? What's our angle? What would get through to her?

Having thought it all through under the watchful eyes of Wise and Medhi…

Masato concluded…!

"R-right, we've gotta find Porta, and we'll figure out what to do once we do— Oh."

Just as he was punting the problem down the road, having found no solution…!

His gaze had wandered, aimlessly looking down the hall toward the corner—

"Wah! They saw me again!"

—and Porta's face was peering around it. Their eyes met!

"Porta! Why are you here?! Coming to check on us is one thing, but you can't let yourself be seen! You've gotta hide better!"

"You shut up! Us finding her is a *good* thing!"

"Hurry, chase after her! We can't lose sight of her again!"

"R-right…uh, but the teacher said not to run in the halls…"

""On your marks…get set…go!""

Leaving Masato in the wind, the girls raced off. "If you go that fast, I can see your panties!" "Then don't look!" "Your own fault if you do!" Ignoring his pleas, they let their skirts flare all the way out! Today was blue and white, respectively!

"Porta! Wait up!"

"We won't do anything violent, so let us catch you!"

"No! I won't be caught! If I get caught, I can't protect my mommy!"

"Man, Porta's fast! There's no way we'll ever catch her! We should just give up and—"

""DASH!""

"Okay…"

Porta raced through the halls, her natural quickness carrying her along.

She drew ahead of them, then abruptly turned and entered a room on one side of the corridor.

Masato and the girls caught up to find a door with the number IV on it.

"This is a Heavenly King's bedroom," said Wise. "Like in the last hideout..."

"She's going to fight us in her room?" asked Medhi.

"Then we'd better be careful. This is Porta's domain! Who knows what sorts of traps she's set...? Take it slow, take it easy, carefully plan a strategy..."

""CHARGE!"" *Slam.*

"Yeah, I figured that would happen."

Wise slammed the door open without a trace of caution, and she and Medhi burst into the room. Masato was forced to follow them.

This was definitely Porta's bedroom. It looked exactly like the image Sorella had shown them. A vast room with nothing in it save a table and a bed.

But there was no sign of Porta herself.

"Think she's hiding somewhere?" wondered Masato.

"Probably. I'd wager the closet, personally."

"But perhaps she just wants us to think that and she's actually used an item to disguise herself."

"And she had that Thou Dost Not Wish to Fight Water. An item to avoid enemy encounters could be used to keep us from noticing her."

Maybe she was only pretending to hide but was actually right next to them!

If they started searching the room, Porta might be planning on slipping out behind them the second they stepped away from the door! Maybe even lock it behind them, trapping them here!

"Right, then it's time for my big bro sensor! Activating sensor...now!"

Masato activated his big bro sensor. This allowed him to locate his adorable little sister no matter where she was! Because he was her big bro!

Imagining where Porta's face might be—"Here!"—he tickled her cheeks!

"I gotcha, Porta! ...Ha-ha, I guess it's not gonna be *that* easy..."

"Eeeep! That tickles!"

"Whaa?! She's actually here?!"

Porta appeared, reeling from the cheek assault!

"Nice, Masato! You're amazing! That was only a little creepy!"

"To summarize: incredibly creepy!"

"Nobody asked for a summary! ...Anyway, I caught her! I caught you, Porta!"

"Eeeep! I-I'm not caught yet!" Porta slipped out of tickle hell and ran to the bed. "I guess I have to fight! Masato! Wise! Medhi! I'll take you on!"

"Fight... No, wait, Porta! You can't mean that!"

"Calm down a minute! Why would we ever fight you? That makes no sense!"

"It does make sense! If I win, I'll be able to protect my mommy! So...!"

"Ah...Masato, Wise, careful!"

Porta took a bottle of glittering liquid out of her shoulder bag and sprinkled it on the stuffed animals on her bed.

They all sprang to life and began charging toward the party!

"Yikes...seriously?! ...I guess they are just stuffed animals, though."

"Hate to break it to you, but this is a futile gesture. Oh well! Guess I'll just blow them all away with my magic!"

The moment Wise pulled out her magic tome...

Porta called out an order. "Cheetah! Go!"

The stuffed cheetah ran very quickly, jumping on Wise's face!

"Wah! Hey, stop that! I can't chant when you... Oh, but...your fur is really soft..."

"Why are you grinning like an idiot?! Don't go getting your magic sealed *physically!*"

"There's no saving her now... It falls to me to put these animals to rest."

Medhi raised her staff.

Porta didn't let that pass unnoticed.

"Whoa! She's casting a death spell! Alpaca, stop her!"

The alpaca charged, leaping on Medhi's face!

"Mmph?! Hey, stop mphat! Now I can't... Oh...but you are terrifyingly mmoft..."

"Medhi's trapped in a plush cage, too... Well done, Porta. But I won't be so easily bested!"

Masato hesitated for a moment but made up his mind and drew the Holy Sword Firmamento!

He held it tightly in both hands, but...

"Huh? This doesn't feel like the way we do things, but... Oh well!"

He was in the middle of a fight. He wasn't about to point his sword at Porta, but he fixed his gaze on his real opponents.

"Sorry, but I've never been a stuffed animal fan. I can slice them apart effortlessly."

"If you do that, I'll feel so bad for the poor animals! Masato, you meanie! You're making me sad!"

"Argh...this is fatal...!"

Porta's voice was sapping Masato's fighting spirit! A powerful debuff! Porta's attacks were too powerful!

"I don't want to put you in any danger, but I have to protect Mommy! Stuffed animals, get him!"

"Argh...well, if I use the flat of the blade, I won't cut them!"

A dozen stuffed animals hurled themselves at Masato.

The first to reach him was a penguin. He knocked it aside with his blade. It was just a stuffed animal—extremely light. It flew all the way to the wall.

"Piece of cake! Okay, next...!"

But the moment his eyes turned to the other animals...

The penguin ricocheted off the wall like a bouncy ball, rocketing toward the side of Masato's head. A direct, fluffy hit!

"Mmph! Yo, what...? That is really soft! Thanks!"

It was a direct hit, but that felt more like a reward! When the penguin went flying off again, he accidentally thanked it.

Masato saw a turtle approaching next and batted it away. Then came an elephant, a dolphin, and a cow, one after another. Each made soft little sounds as they ricocheted. "This is kinda fun!" Super fun.

And the results...

"Ha-ha-ha! Like I said, piece of cake! ...Wait...huh?"

The stuffed animals he knocked away were bouncing off the walls, the floor, and the ceiling, popping back at him.

And it kinda seemed like they got faster every time they bounced. Like terrifyingly fast stuffed pinballs...attacking from all directions...

"Oof?! Blegh…augh? H-hang on a second?!"

"Wah! Mm! Ah-ha! This is…oh, such bliss!"

"Eep! Hyah! Mmph! So fluffyyy!"

"Hey, girls! I get it, but could you *not* wallow in it? They are actually starting to drain our HP here…*damn* it!"

It was time to stop pitying them. Masato changed his grip on the sword and aimed the blade at the chicken coming toward him.

But it didn't cut like he expected—it simply bounced off. In the right circumstances, cotton's extreme bounciness created so much friction, it was harder to cut than iron.

"Sheesh, never figured stuffed animals would be such a threat…"

"Stuffed animals are cute! Cute is powerful!"

"That's you in a nutshell, Porta! But if that's what's going on here… well, we can't hold back anymore! You ready for this, Porta?"

"Yes! I'm ready for anything! I have an ultimate attack ready! This will end things! Here goes!"

"No, I'd prefer you keep holding back, actually."

Porta took the little doll off her shoulder bag—Piita.

Then she took out a bottle of glittering liquid. "One Fight!" she said, and put the bottle to Piita's lips, making it drink.

The liquid seeped into Piita…and then with a *thump*, its body began pulsating. The palm-sized doll was getting larger and larger.

Soon it was taller than Porta, then Masato, then…

"…Yo…this can't be happening…"

"Wha…th-this is…"

"That is *far* too big."

"This is Piita's fighting form! Pretty Prodigious Piita!"

The ceiling in the room was so high, you had to strain to see it, but even when the doll bumped its head on the ceiling, it kept growing.

Leaning farther and farther forward, Pretty Prodigious Piita loomed over them…equally terrifying in both size and position.

"Uh…uh, Porta? Hang on a sec, here."

"W-Wise is right… Let's stop for a moment… This is really worrisome…"

"Piita's attack! Ultimate pile-on!"

"Doesn't sound like an ultimate move but holy craaaaaaap?! Stopppp!!"

Piita's massive body swayed…then toppled toward them.

All three party members tried to scramble away. "Bff?!" "Hey!" "Mm!" But the stuffed animal pinball was ongoing and knocking them backward.

Unable to escape, there was a soft *fooomp* and Piita landed on top of them.

That ended the battle...

"Y-yes! I won! ...Huh?"

Feeling like she'd done something very bad, Porta hung her head.

Then Piita's giant mass moved, slowly rising up.

Masato and the girls had their hands raised, their legs planted, forcing it backward.

"It ain't over yet! Our battle is just beginning!"

"But that phrasing's definitely over! Hnggg!"

"Wow! You're all okay! Thank goodness... No, wait! I can't believe you survived my ultimate attack! How are you all unharmed?!"

"It's thanks to you, Porta!" said Medhi. "Look!"

The three of them were covered in stuffed animals—the same ones that had been tormenting them.

When the massive Piita had fallen, the stuffed animals had merged together, and their bounciness had softened the blow.

"I knew it all along, Porta!" said Masato. "You say you want to fight, but you didn't want to hurt us, either!"

"Th-that's...true, but..."

"Then let's stop all of this! You don't have to fight us."

"But...but if I don't fight...if I don't drive you off...I can't not do that! I have to protect my mommy!"

Porta broke into a run. Ignoring their cries, she headed straight for the door. Like she was running away.

But then Piita stirred. "Whoa...!" One big hand blocked the door, not letting Porta pass.

"Piita...why... Whoaaaa?!"

Piita had stopped trying to pile on the party. It jumped up, reached out its other hand, and scooped Porta up, hugging her to its belly.

"Ooooh...Piita caught me..."

"I feel like something similar happened once before... Wasn't there a giant girl?" asked Wise.

"Porta's so cute, anyone would want to hug her," said Medhi. "Now..."

"That's enough. Porta, we need to talk."

They gathered around, eyes at her level. Porta reluctantly nodded.

Masato himself wasn't really sure what to do here. He had nothing in mind.

So he just ran on impulse.

"First, I want to clear something up. We aren't here to defeat your mom, Porta."

"Huh? …Y-you aren't?!"

"Nope! We're here for *you*," said Wise. "We came to see you, Porta. We were worried."

"You just vanished without explaining anything! Of course we were worried sick," said Medhi.

"You were…worried about me? I-I'm sorry! I didn't mean to worry you…"

Still in Piita's embrace, Porta bowed her head. Such a nice, honest girl.

And that made Masato smile.

"So we're not your enemies, okay?"

"Yes! I was all wrong. I didn't need to fight you! I'm sorry."

"Mm, good. But I'll be honest, we're a little mad at your mom."

"Huh…?"

It hurt to see her look so scared, but Masato wasn't about to stop now.

"We've been given a glimpse of what it's like for you here. I dunno how it works, but Sorella was recording things… Uh, don't worry, I didn't see the part where you changed clothes."

"That's okay! I don't mind if you see me change, Masato!"

"Gah! That's a delightful thing to hear… But this isn't a laughing matter. It was really sad to watch you eating all alone like that."

"Well…I was a little sad, too…"

"And, like, when you tried to say, 'Good morning' and your mother wouldn't let you…or even look at you. That was just mean. I got real ticked off."

"……!"

"I just don't think that's right," said Masato. "It's all too sad. It's just—!"

"But it's the truth," Porta said, desperately trying to smile.

*　　*　　*

"My mommy…hates me."

That definitely wasn't a smile.

"Back in the real world, she was always like that. She never said good morning. I've never had a conversation where she was looking at me. We never ate together."

"But why…?"

"I don't know. Maybe I did something to make her hate me and I just don't remember. That's all I can think of."

"No, wait, Porta… That can't be true."

"There's no way anyone could hate you, Porta!"

"Yes. It doesn't make sense. You're so cute and thoughtful and you work so hard! What's wrong with any of that?"

"But—my mommy—*hates* me!!"

Her voice came out in sobs, big tears gushing down her cheeks.

"When we started this game, my mommy wouldn't come with me! She just sent me an e-mail saying she would if I was good! But no matter how long I waited, she never came! Because she *hates* me!"

"Wait, Porta. There's gotta be a reason…"

"I thought that! I thought she wasn't coming because there was something she had to do that was more important than spending time with me! I thought she must like that other thing better!"

"Porta, calm down! That's so not true! I'm sure it isn't!"

"It is! I did everything I could to make her like me! I got Masato and Mama to let me join your party, then Wise and Medhi joined, and I worked so hard! But my mommy never came! Because she *hates* me!"

"We all know how hard you try. And I promise you nobody could hate someone like that."

"But Mommy hates me! When I saw the wanted poster and called her, she came…but she was the same as always! So, I…I thought if I tried even harder, for her, where she could see me…then maybe…she wouldn't…she…"

After that, it stopped being words. The sobs just drowned everything else out.

Wise and Medhi just hugged her as tight as they could, stroking her head, rubbing her back.

Masato stared at the ceiling, feeling his eyes getting moist, and hoping the tears wouldn't come.

......*But what now?*

He had one idea. Something he'd felt while battling Porta.

He knelt down in front of her, speaking softly.

"Porta, hearing you talk like this...well, now I've got an even bigger problem with your mom."

"It's not my mommy's fault! She's not a bad person! Please forgive her!"

"I can't. Look, everything she's done with the Libere Rebellion? We can forget that. What I can't get past is the way she treats you. I can't do nothing while someone treats a member of my party like this."

"I'm fine! I can handle it! So—!"

"You're not fine, though."

The desperation on her face was painful to look at. He cupped her cheeks—"Hah!" "Mpphhh?!"—and gave them a good squeeze while he wiped her tears.

He then gave her his best brotherly smile.

"So we're gonna do something. Your feelings will be our weapon."

"Huh? They will?"

"Yep. If she won't look at you, we'll make her. We'll just hit her with an emotional bomb."

"B-but..."

"No buts. You've been on all our adventures, Porta. You know that's how we've always solved this kind of problem. We turn sadness into joy. Like we did with Wise, and with Medhi. Right?"

He shot them an impish smile.

They both puffed up their chests proudly.

"Yep! I hit my dumb mom with everything I had! I slammed her with a daughter's feelings!"

"As did I. Although I forget if it was a blow from my tail or the dragon breath that did the trick."

"Probably both. You landed a bunch of critical hits. But well, let's forget about any mistakes that were made... Porta, I know a lot's happened, and you panicked and maybe you forgot how we do things. But this is how we got where we are now. Remember?"

"Y-yes! I remember! I remember now!"

Porta was nodding. The sadness had faded, and her eyes were sparkling again.

Masato took his hands away from her cheeks.

"Okay, Porta. Ready to go hit your mom with all those emotions?"

"My emotions... Mommy..."

"What do you want to tell her?"

She didn't hesitate.

"I want... I want my mommy to love me! I've never been able to tell her that, so I really want to lay it on her!"

A typically Porta-like expression of utmost earnestness, words conveying distilled purity.

It was like they finally had the old Porta back. "She's gonna be fine."

"Seems like it." Wise and Medhi finally released the supportive hugs.

Even giant Piita seemed relieved. It let go of her and reverted to its original size.

Porta put it back in her shoulder bag and nodded.

"Masato! I'm ready to go! I want to go see Mommy right now! I want to hit her with my feelings!"

"Oh, you're all fired up! That's great, Porta. So...I'd love to do that, but I also have some bad news."

"Wh-what bad news?"

"All this time, we've overcome our problems with the full power of the party. The five of us, Mom included. It was all of us together that solved everything. But right now...it's just the three of us."

"Oh, right. Three..."

"Myself, Masato, Wise. Three of us."

"Whaaat? I-I'm not in the party? I'm...oh!"

Porta finally noticed Masato's meaningful stare.

She was still wearing the Libere coat. "I'll go change!" She dashed over to her closet and started undressing...

"...Masato." *Glare.*

"...Masato." *Glare.*

"Porta said she doesn't mind! ...Er, yeah, I suppose that's not the point. Okay."

Masato turned right and savored the sounds instead. That was stimulation enough, and he thoroughly enjoyed himself. No, wait...

He was supposed to be steeling his nerves.

"Uh, Masato, tell me—do we actually have a shot at this?"

"Honestly, I dunno. I've been doing my best to think of a plan...but part of me thinks we'd be better off just letting Porta's pure emotions do the heavy lifting. So let's do that."

"I think that's a wise choice. Porta's purity is the ultimate weapon."

"Yeah. I don't know what her mom's like, but no way she can ignore feelings that powerful. Like, even my mom got it eventually."

"Even my extremely stubborn mother understood by the time the dust settled."

"My mom's ridiculous in her own way...but she's always been a mom. She knows how her son feels."

But as each of their thoughts turned to their mothers...

A shiver ran down their spines.

"Erk...I just got a really bad feeling...b-but maybe I'm just imagining things! Mothers always know how their kids feel! They'd never... never, you know, just hypothetically speaking, do anything that would drive their children to the brink of despair! Ha-ha-ha!"

"N-no, never! Ah-ha-ha!"

"Definitely not! Heh-heh-heh!"

The party forced some smiles.

But reality was far crueler.

Back at the Adventurers Guild in Catharn...

Shiraaase appeared in the doorway, clad in a business suit.

"What name should I give this time...? Shiiirase? Shirararassse? No...I think I'll go with the mysterious producer-slash-manager, Shirase-P!"

Shirase-P named herself to no one in particular, or perhaps the world at large. She stepped outside, a massive overstuffed backpack on her shoulders.

"All right, everyone!" Shirase-P called, addressing the building. "To save the world and see your children in the process! A great adventure awaits! Let's give it all we've got!"

Kazuno and Medhimama peered around the doorway, scowling.

"W-wait, Shiraaase...you can't be serious?"

"Shiraaase? Who might that P? I am the producer/manager extraordinaire, Shirase-P!"

"Oh, God, she's replacing random words with *P*... Are you seriously going to make us do this?"

"It wasn't my idea! This is a proposal from the queen herself! The disturbances in the earth and ocean are caused by the unnatural independent streak in children around the world. The best way to stabilize the children is to turn the children's hearts back toward their mothers!"

"I mean, I understand the logic, but..."

"But this is too much! It's just stupid!"

"Not at all. It's a wonderful idea. There is no better method to convey the wonders of mothers to children and the world. Come on out, you two! Your audience awaits!"

Indeed, a crowd of adventurers was gathering. "Mm? What's up?" "Something going on?" The Adventurers Guild was the hub of any adventurer's life—they were never in short supply.

Kazuno and Medhimama were looking paler by the moment.

"Y-you're kidding. We really have to show ourselves in public dressed like this?"

"K-Kazuno...you couldn't accidentally cast a transport spell? We could run away together!"

"Great idea! Let's do this... *Transportare!* ...Argh, my magic isn't working...because Shirase-P has my magic tome..."

"Why did you let her take it?! She took all my gear, too, leaving me without a single spell!"

"Wait, wait, wait, wait! Seriously, wait! If I go out in public like this... and if that dumb daughter of mine sees me wearing this outfit..."

"P-perish the thought! If Medhi saw me like this, I wouldn't just pass out, I'd die instantly!"

"Don't worry! I'm sure Ma-kun and your girls will be delighted! I can already see them waving their glowsticks!"

"Please, as if that would ever happen! ...Wait..."

"Augh! Mamako! Don't...!"

From the back of the Adventurers Guild, moving like the wind...

Dancing out before Shirase-P and the adventurers...

"My love is boundless! I love you sooo much! Let me give you a biiig hug! I'm Mom Idol Number One, Mamako Oosuki! Hee-hee-hee."

Wearing an adorable top and a short frilly skirt...

There was Mamako with her cute smile and a flirty wink. ☆

In the darkest hour appears a mom idol to impart how wonderful mothers are!

"Hello, everyone! …Oh? No answer?"

This was all too sudden. The crowd of adventurers were frozen in silence.

Shirase-P nodded.

"You show up full of excitement and anticipation, but the audience is unmoved. That is how debuts go! This is a road every idol must walk down. It all starts here!"

"Right, Shirase-P! I'll do my best! Hee-hee-hee!"

"Now there's a beautiful smile! I love the enthusiasm. You're the leader, the heart of the idol group, so please take center stage—and strike a symmetrical pose."

"Like this?"

She spread both arms, as if waiting for a dive into Mommy's bosom. "Perfect!" Shirase-P gave it the seal of approval.

"Next, Idols two and three! Come on out! The longer you keep us waiting, the more adventurers will arrive. Which works well from a strategic perspective…"

"Argh…f-fine! I just have to get it over with!"

"We agreed to do the job. And if Mamako's so confident, I'm not about to be outdone! Ever!"

Fueled by irritation and a competitive spirit, Kazuno and Medhimama finally stepped through the door.

"Neither of us are honest with our feelings! You got a problem with me? Spit it out! Family squabbles are my thing! I'm Mom Idol Number Two, Night Queen! Quit your ogling!"

"Being strict is an expression of love! Side by side with the children, we'll strive for greater heights! I'm Mom Idol Number Three, Medhimama! Oh-ho-ho!"

Clad in idol costumes that matched Mamako's, the other two mom idols took their positions at her side, striking poses!

Kazuno went for the "Come at me!" delinquent pose. Nailed it.

Medhimama went for the strict-and-brainy class president look. Nailed it.

But the crowd was still just gaping at them in silence.

"Argh…kill me! Kill me now!"

"Kazuno, no idol would ever speak like that. Be proud! We can't pull back now."

Tears were streaming down both their cheeks, but Shirase-P started clapping for them.

"Well done, you two! ...If I had my druthers, you'd have gone for a more idol-like 'Tee-hee ☆' but..."

"Don't push it! Consider how old we are! If we tried that, the audience would puke blood!"

"Hee-hee-hee. Don't worry. We can do it if we try! Tee-hee! ☆"

"That worked?! ...W-well, maybe if you look as young as Mamako..."

"Mamako can do it... Very well, I've made up my mind. I've just got to act like an idol...like an idol...tee...tee...tee-haghhh?!" Blood puke.

"See? I knew it! Memama! Hang in there! Although your wounds are severe and you're probably doomed!"

"Hmm...well, in that case I shall leave it up to your best judgment and your individual personalities. We don't have much time, so let's get started."

With Shirase-P in the lead, the moms began to take their leave.

"Shirase-P, what is our idol group's name?" asked Mamako.

"Oh, right! We hadn't picked one yet. Let's think about it as we go."

"Uh, is this really the time? Memama's in critical condition!"

"Kazuno...I don't think I can make it... Just leave me here..."

"No, you're definitely coming! No way I'm letting you wriggle out of it this easy!"

"Argh...group solidarity is a thorn in my side..."

The mom idol group walked away, before the stunned stares of the silent crowd. A sad launch—but they had much to accomplish.

Someday, they would be on a shining stage, basking in the cheers of their fans...

All in order to save the world, and to be reunited with their beloved children.

"Ma-kun...Mommy's coming! Just you wait!" Mamako whispered, gazing up at the sky.

She envisioned Masato's smile...and his eyes rolling back in his head and an anguished expression on his face, but surely that part was just her imagination.

Mom Roster Profile 3

Medhimama

■Age:
It's rude to ask a woman her age. You should know better.

■Hobbies:
Acquiring credentials via correspondence courses. I don't plan on actually using what I've learned, but working hard to pass each course provides me with a sense of constant personal growth.

■Specialties:
Massages, I suppose. They're good for health and beauty, and my daughter seemed to appreciate them.

■Best Feature:
I've always been fond of the beauty mark below my lip.

■Childhood Dream:
I had a teacher I admired a great deal, so I wanted to be a teacher myself once. That was so long ago.

■Catchphrase:
"Fortitude and resolve." Be steadfast in your beliefs and firm in your decisions. This is vital to rearing children.

■Child-Rearing Philosophy:
I believe parents ought to strictly monitor their children's studies and personal lives. There are limits to this, however.

■To Your Beloved Child:
To my beloved daughter,

Are you doing well? I'm sure you are living a life of principle and experiencing an archetypal adventure. Know that I am proud of you for this, as your mother.

You are the greatest daughter.

With all my love, yours truly.

Chapter 4 Something's Happening Without Our Knowledge. Something Outrageous.

The crystal ball on the desk was showing a live feed of Masato's party running around Deathmother Castle.

"I'm definitely getting chills, here...b-but no matter! We've gotta reach Porta's mom! Is this the right way?"

"Yes! Straight down there to the throne...huh? The door's gone!"

"The passage leads to a dead end where a door clearly should be, but there isn't one... Oh, maybe she doesn't want to meet—"

"No, Wise. She's just being cautious, since we are infiltrating her lair."

"R-right! Good point, Medhi. That must be it!"

"In that case...let's check our surroundings thoroughly! Commence investigation!"

"Okay! I'll look over here... Eep, monsters!"

Porta was happily running around, back with her companions, who were looking after her and supporting her. They were about to enter combat, and everyone was bracing themselves, but...

In a chair elsewhere in the castle, watching their every move, Porta's mother found her heart at peace.

"Yes. That's how it should be. That's where you belong."

Dark-Mom Deathmother looked content. She'd looked like this since retiring to her chambers. Her eyes never left the crystal ball, as if she didn't want to miss a single one of Porta's actions or expressions.

This was Dark-Mom Deathmother's happy time. If only it could last forever.

But no sooner had that thought crossed her mind than there was a knock at her door.

"...Oh, yes. This always happens," she muttered.

She waved a hand, dismissing the image in the crystal. Her expression hardened into that of a demon lord.

"Enter," she said, not even glancing at the door.

It was Hahako, looking a little embarrassed.

"Sorry. I interrupted again, didn't I?"

"So be it. I'm used to it by now. But...you're still here? I've removed the restrictions, so you may go where you wish."

"...You're sure?"

"I am. You did exactly as I'd hoped. I appreciate your escorting her companions here. Your freedom is my way of thanking you. You might want to rescue those poor children from their two-hundredth attempt at escaping the game of traps. Whether they accept you as a mother or not."

"About that..." Hahako began. She seemed gravely worried. "Is it true that children don't need parents?"

"It is," Dark-Mom Deathmother replied. No trace of hesitation. "A strategy based on my ideas is rapidly advancing in every corner of the world. Children everywhere are leaving their parents and living fine lives on their own. See it with your own eyes."

She waved a hand at the crystal. The outside world appeared...

"Oh my!"

".........Huh.........?"

...but the sight made Hahako yelp with delight, and Dark-Mom Deathmother's glasses fell off her face.

The world was in danger.

What had started with a tiny shift had expanded until all the world knew about it. The same thing was happening everywhere.

"All right, my next delivery is... Yikes?! Whoaaa!"

A wagon traveling between towns suddenly lost its balance, toppling over.

It had tumbled into a sudden depression in the ground. Other travelers quickly ran to help.

"This again?! How many times...!"

"I dunno! There was just one on the other road!"

"Hey! We need help over here! The ships in the harbor are in trouble!"

"It's everywhere!"

Land and sea alike were in big trouble.

A depression had appeared by the docks, and the ships at anchor were all falling in.

The fishermen had ropes attached and were desperately trying to haul their ships back out…but were on the verge of getting yanked into the ocean themselves.

"Let go! You can't save it!"

"We got no choice! Our trade depends on it! Without this ship, we can't eat tomorr—augh?!"

"Crap! He fell in! Someone throw a life preserver!"

Depressions in the earth and ocean alike.

Appearing with no warning, throwing lives into turmoil.

"Damn it…what's going on? How is this even possible?"

"Does anyone know anything?! What is the world coming to?!"

The cause of the phenomenon had already been discovered. And the Queen of Catharn had instructed that this be made public knowledge the world over.

But officials scrambling to handle the constant incidents had no time to check the reports. Vital documents were sitting untouched on their desks.

With no knowledge of the countermeasures, the damage spread unchecked.

"It's like the end of the world… Are we doomed?!"

Despair spread through the crowd.

The end of the world. Words that inspired fear, sadness, and regret. People fell to their knees, faces buried in hands.

But…

"Pardon the interruption at such a busy juncture. May I have a moment of your time? I can info-P you that this is my card."

"Huh? …Shirase-P?"

In their darkest moment, a producer/manager appeared out of nowhere, carrying a backpack and a shoulder bag. With no regard to the crisis at hand, she began handing out business cards.

"I am here today to introduce you all to a new idol group our company is actively promoting."

"No, um…this really isn't the time…"

"Oh, come now. It will only take a moment, and I assure you—they're a feast for the eyes."

"No, like…seriously, not right now! We're dealing with an emergency! It's the end of the world!"

"Don't worry! The world will not end. We're here to save it!"

"Huh…?"

Strong. Kind. Warm. Reliable. Just hearing her voice made you feel safe.

The people looked up to see the promising new idol group running over. First…

"Being strict is an expression of love! Side by side with the children, we'll strive for greater heights!! I'm Mom Idol Number Three, Medhimama! Oh-ho-ho!"

Medhimama looked confident—she'd made her peace with this whole thing.

"Neither of us are honest with our feelings! You got a problem with me? Spit it out! Family squabbles are my thing! I'm Mom Idol Number Two, Night Queen! Quit your ogling."

She was still slightly embarrassed by this whole situation, but she was counting on enthusiasm to get her through it—Kazuno knew that nerves make the woman.

Both struck a pose. And between them…

"My love is boundless! I love you sooo much! Let me give you a biiig hug! I'm Mom Idol Number One, Mamako Oosuki! Hee-hee-hee."

Mamako's smile was so enthusiastic, it was clear she was enjoying every second of this.

The three of them spoke together.

""""Together, we're MOM-3! Are you all being good children?!""""

Announcing the name of their group, each of them smiled—one gentle, one looking for a fight, one super strict. Blinding! Shining! Legitimate idols!

And as always, this left everyone dumbfounded.

Shirase-P applauded their performance. Producer-approved.

"Very good! You're definitely starting to seem like idols! The group name is clearly critical. Now your hearts will become one, and you'll only get more into it as time passes!"

"Yes. I do feel like the three of us can do it together!"

"I'm more crying inside because there's no way out now…"

"Kazuno, you are forbidden from griping about this further. We have no choice."

"I know, I know, jeez… You old windbag…"

"Say that *again*, Kazuno? *What* did you call me?" An ominous rumbling followed.

"Right, now that the group name is settled, and everyone's ready to go, it's time to start resolving the world's problems! Everyone, prepare your Idol Sensors!"

""".......What?""""

Clearly, none of the mom idols had the slightest idea what Shirase-P was talking about.

"Idol Sensors...a special skill only mom idols have! It allows you to seek out the stage where you will shine brightest as an idol! And where your activities are needed—in other words, where parent-child problems exist! Let's all head where your Sensors take us! Come!"

".......Is that a real skill?"

"I think she's goofing around again..."

"Well, it can't hurt to try. Like this?"

Mamako focused her mind and held out a hand, trying to detect family problems that might lie in that direction.

Looking very dubious, Kazuno and Medhimama followed Mamako's lead, aiming their hands in different directions.

Did they sense anything...?

"...Mm? Huh?"

Kazuno was the first to speak.

"Do you sense something, Kazuno?"

"Uh...well, I think a mom is arguing with her daughter? It kinda feels like me and Genya... Over there."

"Amazing! The skill really works! Shirase-P, I apologize for my earlier rudeness. You were absolutely correct."

"No, no, I am every bit as surprised. I just made it up, you see."

""""What?!""""

"Just talking to myself. Never you mind. Kazuno, can you pinpoint the source? We have little time and should get to work right away."

"Pinpoint...oh. I feel like I've been there before... Yes, I know. We can get there with a teleportation spell. Can I have my tome?"

Shirase-P handed a magic tome to Kazuno, who muttered, "*Transportare!*" Her cast cancel skill allowed her to skip the rest of the chant, so that was all it took to activate the teleportation spell.

The four of them were bathed in the spell's light, their gleaming outfits shining even brighter—and then they flew away.

"They were like angels...no, goddesses! Have we witnessed a miracle?!"

"I feel like something good will happen…they might actually…"

The light of hope came back to the downcast crowd as the mom idols flew away.

The ball of light carried the mom idols to the entrance of a village.

Before them were fields and rice paddies, horses and cows out to pasture—a pastoral idyll. Were it not for the depressions everywhere, the town seemed peaceful.

"Oh my! This is Maman Village!"

"Yep. This is where I sensed the problem. Personally, I don't have the best memories of the place…and I can't tell you which house or which parent and child are having problems."

"Then we'll just have to ask around."

"No, wait—there's no need to take up that much time," Shirase-P said.

"You're going to make something up again, aren't you? Can't you be serious for one minute?" Medhimama demanded.

"Fear not. This time it's a legitimate technique. If you're looking for someone, it's better to call them to you. As idols, you have that powerful appeal."

"Idol power calls people to us? I suppose that *does* sound like an idol thing. But…how, specifically?" asked Kazuno.

"You're idols! Sing and dance."

Shirase-P began rummaging through her luggage and took out a small machine covered in levers and knobs, with a morning-glory-shaped trumpet on top.

"This is a digital phonograph. Not only can it play music files, it also allows recording and mixing! Isn't that splendid? I will sample a few sounds and apply them to the included rhythm patterns, creating music. You will then sing and dance to it! Go ahead!"

MOM-3: Stand by!

"No, no, no, no, that's ridiculous!"

"Yes! We have taken neither dancing nor singing lessons! We can't just…!"

"Let your feelings carry you."

"We can't!"

"No way! Absolutely not!"

"Oh, really? It seems like one of you already is."

Shirase-P glanced behind them.

Kazuno and Medhimama both turned to look.

"Hmm-hmm, hmm-hmm-hmmm... And then I turn like so...oh, should I do a 'there, there' or a 'good, good' here? I just can't decide! Hee-hee-hee."

Leaves drifting on the breeze. Birds chirping. Matching these peaceful sounds...

Mamako let her body move to the rhythm, humming a melody, whispering the lyrics.

She'd become a forest mom idol. Like a musical mom spirit.

As Shirase-P quietly began recording, Kazuno and Medhimama stared, entranced.

"Mamako...you're amazing..."

"We can't match her. But...I find myself wanting to try..."

"That's the spirit! Let's get started! Guerrilla concerts in the middle of the street are what new idol groups are all about!"

"Yes, then—no, we can't let her get us! Some things are simply impossible!"

"Does this even count as a street?! We're surrounded by farms! There's nothing here but grasshoppers and frogs!"

Kazuno and Medhimama returned to their senses and attempted to release themselves from Shirase-P's grasp, but before they could...

"I don't need a mom! I can manage just fine without you! Bye-bye!"

"You foolish child! Come back here! Why won't you listen to your mother?!"

A mother's and daughter's voices raised in anger.

A five-year-old girl came racing out of the village, running toward them. Short pigtails held in place with decorative bunny faces. Definitely seemed the impish type.

The mother running after her was clearly still quite young, but neither was really looking where she was going...

"Aaand...bump!" *Thunk.*

"Eeek!"

Kazuno made no effort to avoid the child at all, letting the girl run straight into her and knocking her down.

Kazuno then grabbed a pigtail in each hand and hauled her to her feet.

"Pedal to the metal. Vroom vroom. Kidding!"

"Hey! Those aren't handles! And quit acting like my mom!"

"Ah-ha-ha! I thought you'd do that. I sure did when I was your age."

The girl was pounding her fists on Kazuno's belly but...she was five, so it was just cute.

Then her mother caught up. The snarl on her youthful face suggested she'd been a wild teenager. She grabbed a fistful of Kazuno's clothes, glaring at her.

"Get your hands off my child!" she roared.

"I helped you out, and this is my thanks? Sounds familiar really... I was so young myself."

"This ain't funny! What the hell does that even mean? Who the hell are you, all dressed up in that ridiculous getup?!"

"I'm just a passing mom idol. Nice to meetcha."

"Huh?! Mom idol?! Have you lost your mind?!... Uh, wait..."

The mother saw the people behind Kazuno, and her eyes went wide.

"M-Mamako! You're Mamako, right?!"

"Yes, I am! You remembered me?"

"Of course I do! When that crazy demon who called herself the Queen of the Night showed up, you saved the village! How could I forget?!"

"Crazy...? Well, I did go a *bit* too far, I admit."

"But, um...Mamako, what are you wearing?"

The mother looked around at Mamako, Kazuno, and Medhimama, all dressed in matching idol costumes.

Then...

"First, let's introduce ourselves! I'm Mom Idol Number One, Mamako Oosuki!"

"And I'm Mom Idol Number Two, Night Quee—ah, to hell with it, Kazuno's fine."

"I'm Mom Idol Number Three, Medhimama."

"Together, we are..."

They rapidly took up their positions.

""""The all-mom idol group, MOM-3!"""""

Tah-dahhh! They struck their signature pose!

The mom and her little girl just gaped at them. A powerful stun effect!

"Three mom idols here to tell everyone how great moms are, restore bonds between parents and children, and save the world! Hee-hee-hee."

"I-I see… Er, actually, I don't really get it, sorry."

"So that's why we wanted to talk to you. It seems like the two of you were fighting. What happened? Do you mind sharing?"

"Uh, sure… My daughter, she just—"

"Don't touch me!"

The mother had reached for her daughter, but her hand was slapped away.

"Ow! What's your problem?"

"Shut up, Mom! I'm done with you and your constant scolding! You're not my mom anymore!"

"I'm not scolding you! I just said that pin is dangerous, and you should take it off!"

"Nuh-uh! It's cute! All my friends have them! I'm keeping it! If you want me to take it off, then you have to do what I say!"

"Don't be so selfish! Just listen to me—!"

"Yeah, yeah, that's enough," Kazuno interrupted. "We ain't got time to listen to you squabble. Give us the short version."

The mother scowled at her, and then turned to Mamako.

"I'm sorry to be a bother, Mamako."

"Oh, I promise you aren't."

"Why are you polite to her and not me? Psh, whatever."

"Anyway, you can see what she's like. She found these dangerous pins somewhere and stuck them in her hair and insists she won't take them off unless I do what she says. She wants me to fix the broken hot springs."

"Fix the hot springs? What does that mean? Isn't the hot springs Maman Village's main attraction?"

"Yes, but the water in the hot springs stopped being hot. Since every house in the village is connected to the hot springs, none of us can take a bath at all. So…"

"A mom who can't even run a bath is good for nothing! If I'm just wiping myself down with a wet cloth, I can do that by myself! I don't need a mom anymore!"

"There she goes again! Stop that!"

The girl stuck out her tongue and ran off. The mother gave chase, genuinely furious. "Come back here!" "No way!" They ran around and around the mom idols, like a game of tag.

So…

"What do we do?" asked Mamako.

"Let's assess the situation. Memama, can you bring us up to speed?"

"Ahem. First, the children are growing arrogant under the influence of these pins. To restore parent-child relationships, the pins must be removed. But this child has proposed a condition for said removal. Specifically, the restoration of the hot springs. If we can achieve this goal, there is no guarantee the child will keep her end of the bargain, but it seems we have no choice but to attempt the repair. That is all."

"So first, we repair the hot springs? It does seem like a problem for everyone, so let's take care of it!"

"You make it sound easy, Mamako, but how do we do that? If there's only cold water, there must be a problem underground somewhere..."

"Assuming this has something to do with the diminishing influence of Mother Earth seems reasonable," Shirase-P said, sneaking past the game of mother-daughter tag. "This definitely calls for the mom idols. Leave things to us! Producer/manager extraordinaire, Shirase-P, will prepare the perfect stage for you all! Heh-heh-heh!"

"Wow...that's not gonna end well, is it?"

Kazuno shuddered. But Shirase-P was staring right at her...

The hot water used in every Maman Village home came from the main spring at the edge of town.

Like a naturally formed well, it would normally have steam rising off of it. Since hot water was flowing continually from it, if you touched it, you'd burn yourself. But now only cold water was coming out.

And that ice-cold main spring was the stage for the mom idol concert.

Shirase-P was checking the music machine when the Maman Village chief approached her.

"Um, Shirase-P, was it? Do you have a moment? I can't help but notice the idol group you've brought with you has a certain demon in it. One who attacked our village, calling herself the Queen of the Night."

"Never fear! I'm sure you know that incident was resolved peacefully. The Queen of the Night has turned over a new leaf and is now a wonderful mother in her own right. There is no cause for alarm."

"I-I suppose not. And, well…Mamako's with her, so…fine. I'll leave this in your hands, and we will simply watch over the results."

The chief bowed and went back to the other villagers.

The entire village had gathered around the spring. Not just the mother and daughter they'd met at the village entrance, but everyone, young and old, male and female—and horse and cow.

Plenty of other parents had brought their kids. All the children were wearing the pins the Libere Rebellion had scattered around and were acting unnaturally independent, trying to leave their parents' sides. But their parents had firm grasps on their collars and were keeping them in place.

The stage was set. The audience had gathered. Everything was ready.

"Then let's begin! Music, start!"

Shirase-P flipped the switch on the digital phonograph, and in time with the preset rhythm, birds chirped, cows mooed, and horses whinnied. These sounds she'd gathered on-site created a very relaxed tune.

MOM-3, the all-mom idol group, was here!

"Ta-da! Hello, everyone! Nice to see you again. Today I'm here as Mom Idol Number One, Mamako Oosuki!"

Mamako came running out from behind a tree.

Not in her idol costume, but in an old-fashioned school swimsuit!

"Oh! Mamako means business!"

"Mamakoooo! Thanks again! We're so happy to see you!"

"She's in such great shape! I wish I still had her figure."

"Thank you! Thank you, everyone! Hee-hee-hee!"

The crowd was responding well. Perhaps they were more used to seeing swimsuits than idol costumes. Mamako was enthusiastically waving at the audience.

Behind her…

"Why swimsuits?! This makes no sense!"

"I never thought I'd wear one here…and I hate myself for coming prepared…"

Looking extremely unhappy about it, Kazuno and Medhimama stepped out from behind the tree. Also in swimsuits.

Kazuno had a slender figure, much like her daughter. She wore a standard bikini.

Medhimama was wearing the same scandalous adult suit she'd flaunted at the academy pool.

"Idols two and three! Smile! Your fans await."

"You're asking too much! Forcing us to change into swimsuits here...for what?!"

"Don't worry! There's a good reason for it. Mamako's getting the crowd warmed up, so start your idol activities! Go on, Kazuno."

Shirase-P pointed at the main springs, where cold water surged forth.

"Er...me? What do you...?"

"Jump in."

"Huh?! What for?! It's cold! I'll get hypothermia!"

"Oh, I forgot to mention. Make sure you jump in *comically*."

"Are you even listening?! What kind of idol goes around jumping into cold water anyway?! This is more like a two-bit travel documentary. I'm not doing it!"

Kazuno was vehemently opposed. "Then I will!" Mamako raised her hand. "No, I will!" Medhimama did, too. "Then go ahead!" Kazuno stuck to her guns.

Shirase-P leaned in, whispering in her ear. "Any real idol knows sometimes you have to sacrifice yourself for a laugh."

"Not very convincing..."

"Then let's put it this way. This is how you pay for the trouble you caused as the Queen of the Night. Put a little effort into your atonement. You get the crowd all excited, then you warm the water up with your magic, and then you all live happily ever after. How does that sound?"

"Argh...i-if you put it that way...then I guess I have to! Damn it!"

She clearly did feel some guilt. Kazuno gritted her teeth and strode toward the springs.

The villagers watched curiously as she knelt down at the edge of the springs.

"Um...w-wow, that looks cold... Mamako, Memama, don't you dare push—"

"Oh my. Do excuse me." *Shove!*

"I wasn't even done yet! Aughh!!"

Medhimama caught on a little too fast, and Kazuno plunged head-first into the water.

"C-c-c-coooold!"

"Good! Keep it up!" Kazuno looked ready to freeze to death, but Shirase-P just shot her a thumbs-up. No concern for Kazuno's well-being.

"This is outrageous! Are you trying to kill me?! B-but...if this gets the villagers all excited..."

Her nose running, Kazuno looked hopefully toward the crowd.

But they were all just gaping at her.

"Crickets, huh?! Not even smiles?! ...Argh! Fine—if you all won't get heated up, then I'll have to provide the heat! Just rein it in a bit, and... *Flusso di Lava!*"

A massive magic tome appeared in her hand, and the spell activated.

A tiny amount of magma rose up beneath the spring, and the water warmed up immediately.

"Much better! Ooh, that's nice and warm... Well, villagers? What do you say?"

"It's warm... You mean, the hot springs are back?"

"Look! There's steam rising off it! Our hot springs are restored!"

"The mom idols fixed it! MOM-3 is amazing!"

The villagers cheered, gathering around the edge of the spring. They put their hands in the water, making sure the temperature was right, letting out cries of joy.

Mamako and Medhi also slipped into the hot springs, smiling.

"Oh my! The temperature's perfect! Kazuno, good work!" said Mamako.

"Ha-ha! It was light work for me."

"But won't it go back to being cold the moment you undo the spell?" asked Medhimama.

"Yeah. It's just an emergency fix, won't fool anyone but children... but hopefully enough to make these stubborn kids listen to reason."

Kazuno glanced to one side.

The squabbling mother and daughter were nearby.

"So, kid?" Kazuno said. "The hot springs are back. You gonna listen to your mom now?"

"Huh? Uh, umm..."

The girl seemed genuinely surprised. She looked at the water, then Kazuno, then her mother.

Then she hid the bunny pins with both hands, turning her back.

"N-no! Mom didn't fix the hot springs! I'm not taking these off, ever!"

"This again...?"

"Ah-ha-ha!" Kazuno laughed. "Didn't fool her, huh? Oh, well. Fine, then. Do whatever you like."

"Huh...?"

The girl gaped at Kazuno.

"What are you...?" Medhimama hissed.

"Don't worry, it'll be fine," Mamako said, stopping her.

Kazuno had an idea. She was acting like she didn't care, but she was watching the little girl carefully.

"I can keep the pins?"

"Sure. Leave 'em on!"

"What? You can't tell her that! She can't—"

"Sure she can! If kids won't listen, let 'em do what they want. That's one way to resolve these things. That's how I raised my daughter."

Kazuno took her eyes off the kid, gazing up at the sky.

"You're a mother—you know how it goes. We all struggle with our daughters being just like us even in ways we *don't* want them to be. Especially if you're selfish and stubborn—they'll definitely get those in spades, and that guarantees you'll butt heads. Constantly."

"Well...you're right. That hits way too close to home."

"Best way to handle that is to give each other some space until you both cool off. That doesn't mean abandoning her. But if you love your daughter, taking some time apart and waiting until you can speak calmly to her is really important. And if you still can't keep your cool, sometimes you just need to throw down. But that's for another time."

"But if something happens while we're apart..."

"Well, you can always just keep an eye on her. Worry your little heart out, never mind what you're fighting over. It ain't easy to worry about someone you're mad at, but...if you're serious about this mom thing, I'm sure you can do it."

And with that, Kazuno started washing her face. Embarrassed by her own heartfelt speech, she felt her face turn red, so she began splashing hot water on it...which seemed likely to increase her circulation and make her turn even redder.

The mother thought for a moment, and then turned to her daughter.

"Wh-what, Mom? I'm not taking these bunnies off!"

"That's okay. Do what you like. You can do whatever you want."

"Huh? ...I can?"

"But in return, if anything happens because of those pins, I'm not going to help. I'm washing my hands of the whole thing."

With that made clear, the mother refused to say another word.

The girl gave her a long, searching look.

"Then I don't need 'em," she said. She took the bunny pins off her hairbands and threw them to the ground.

"Huh? Er, what? Why'd you...?"

"I said I don't need 'em, so I don't need 'em! Mm!"

"Uh...what...?"

The girl had leaped into her mother's arms and was rubbing her face against her belly. Like a totally spoiled child.

This mother was too young and inexperienced to know what this meant. She just looked confused.

But the mom idols had been through it all and knew exactly how children worked. They'd all seen this coming and were nodding happily.

"Even if the pin makes her try to be mature and push herself, she's still so young—that's as far as it could take things. She was only fighting you because she wanted your attention."

"That's what children do. Hee-hee-hee. Well done, Kazuno."

"Oh, stop. I didn't do a thing."

"That's hardly the case. I mean...look."

Looking around them, things were changing.

Shirase-P was in the water next to Kazuno, in a black bikini. "When did you—?!" "I got changed right away." No matter.

Other children were staring at the little girl and getting jealous. "Mommyyy!"

"Wha...where'd this come from?" One after another, they threw their pins away, and leaped into the embrace of their moms. Or clung to their arms, swinging.

And then the ground began to change, too.

The depressions around them slowly filled in, returning to their original shape.

And not just around the spring, either—all the depressions around Maman Village and beyond were restored. The restoration was spreading far and wide.

"With the unnatural independence resolved, and the mothers' emotions back to normal, Mother Earth has recovered, too. Just as we expected. A brilliant result."

"Nicely done, Kazuno. This one was all yours."

"S-stop that already! I just...I didn't...h-huh?"

As an embarrassed smile flicked across Kazuno's lips, another change occurred—right in front of her.

The steam around them swirled, coalesced...and transformed into a palm-sized crystal. Pulsing with a gentle light, it moved toward Kazuno's bosom—and vanished inside her.

Kazuno obtained the Parental Bond Let Them Be!

"I...seem to have acquired something. Shirase-P, do you know what this is?"

"*Gasp!* I can't believe it... That is your bond with your child, Kazuno! If you follow that bond, it'll take you to your daughter—to the unknown location of the enemy lair! I'm sure it's a quest item."

"You make that sound convincing, but it's a guess, right?" Medhimama scowled.

"It sure is. I just made it up," Shirase-P said with utter confidence. "As we resolve problems in different districts, we'll obtain these quest items! Once we've collected all of them, our path forward will open! Classic RPG design. It is a legitimate possibility."

"Well, if you say so, I'm sure that's how it works, Shirase-P! Hee-hee-hee."

"Then I'll pretend to be convinced. Let's use our Idol Sensors and head to the next location."

"I'll prepare us for departure," said Shirase-P. "...Oh, Kazuno, you can stay where you are just a bit longer. I'm expecting a good reaction on your part."

"Roger that. As a reward for my hard efforts, I'm gonna have a nice long soak... Huh? Reaction?"

Mamako and Medhimama had both stood up and were holding out their hands, concentrating. Shirase-P was busy collecting the audio equipment.

A few moments later, Kazuno leaped out of the water. "Hotttttt!" she yowled, rolling across the ground.

With the power of the earth restored, the hot springs were back to their original temperature: very, very hot. "Ha-ha! That old lady's funny!" "Old?!" Her comedy act had the whole village in stitches. At last her sacrifices had borne fruit. This was how an idol should live!

Meanwhile…

"…Oh, is that…?"

"Medhimama? Have you sensed something?"

"Yes. It's quite clear. Our next destination…is Mahweh. The school town."

Medhimama savored the name and the memories it brought with it.

Once they were done changing, the mom idols said good-bye to the villagers and took a transport spell to Mahweh.

The sight of three moms in idol costumes (and Shirase-P staggering under the weight of her luggage) left the townsfolk frozen in their tracks, mouths agape. Even those who kept moving were so busy staring, they accidentally tumbled into a depression.

The place of learning in the town's center stood as it always had, projecting an air of refined dignity.

"So that's the school…pretty big place, huh? Wow…"

"Your first time here, Kazuno?"

"I saw a photo in one of the reports management sent me on what my idiot daughter was up to."

"I believe this was just another inn town while you were still active in the game, Kazuno. Somebody—I won't say who—made an aggressive plea to management that the game was sorely lacking in educational facilities, and we were forced to make an emergency update adding one. I won't say who."

She didn't say it, but Shirase-P's eyes were certainly locked on the person in question.

"W-well, enough talk! Let's move forward!"

"Ah-ha. Attempting to distract us, I see."

"Ho-ho-ho! I have no idea what you're talking about, Shirase-P. What matters is that somewhere in this town is a problem for us to solve. Where could it be? Oh! The children would be in class at this hour, so we should probably start there."

The unnamed founder of the school, Medhimama, led the group forward, directly toward the school gates.

But as they got closer, things took a baffling turn.

"…Oh, my! What could that mean?"

The school gates were barred with iron fencing.

If this was done to prevent crime, there was nothing wrong with it—but the people the fencing barred from entering were wearing professorial gowns. The school's teachers.

Among the baffled faculty was a large, well-built man.

"Is that… Oh, it is! Mr. Burly."

"Yes! Hello, Mr. Burly."

"Mm? I know that voice…Mamako Oosuki! And…Medhimama?!" Mr. Burly turned around and stared at one mom, then the other.

Also… "Ohhh, you're really *ripped.*" "Uh, thanks…?" …He had one last shocked stare for Kazuno, who had her hands all over him.

"W-well, what a treat!" he bellowed. "The former headmaster-by-proxy, companions! What a lovely sight you are! Gah-ha-ha!"

Seeing the mothers of academy graduates all decked out in idol costumes had been a shock, but he'd overcome it. Mr. Burly's fortitude knew no bounds.

"Welcome, welcome! I can't tell you how pleased I am to see you, Mamako."

"I'm delighted as well! Lovely to see you in such good spirits. It seems like there's rather a lot of teachers gathered here…"

"We've upped our staffing levels! Thanks to your help with our test run, the academy is in full swing, with many more teachers and students. Well, there are still some shortcomings there…"

They looked around the teaching staff again.

More than half the faces were ASCII art—rushed implementations. "We're still extremely short staffed. I do apologize," Shirase-P said on behalf of the management. "No, no, don't worry about it," Mamako insisted.

"Stop right there! That is hardly the point Mamako was trying to make, was it?" Medhimama said, index finger snapping forward. "Say, Mr. Burly. Shouldn't you be in class right now?"

"Y-yes, I should, but…"

"Then why are all the teachers standing outside? This is most peculiar. Highly irregular. Teachers belong in the classroom, instructing their students!"

"I-I'm well aware of that," Mr. Burly said, deflating under the force of Medhimama's wrath. "That is how things should be. But…I'm afraid the students have staged a coup d'état and banished the faculty from the school grounds."

Mr. Burly bowed apologetically.

"...Huh? A coup?!"

"Yes. No armed force was involved, but the students suddenly challenged us to a battle on our individual subjects and..."

"And the teachers lost?!"

"I'm afraid so. We may have underestimated them but...the students' sudden development was simply astounding. As a teacher, I should be delighted...but given the outcome of the battles..."

"You were forced to obey the students and vacate the premises. I cannot believe my ears."

"I make no excuses." Mr. Burly was down on his knees before her.

"Medhimama, perhaps that's enough..." Mamako said. "Mr. Burly, did you notice anything different about the students? Were they, perhaps, wearing some unusual pins?"

"That they were! Not pins for children, more like school crests but...I suspect those were the items the whole town is talking about, the ones that make children grow up too fast."

"If you knew that, why didn't you take them away? Confiscating prohibited items is all part of a teacher's job."

Kazuno was right, and Mr. Burly knew it.

"Our school's mission is to educate would-be adventurers. We actively teach the importance of equipping items that will raise your stats! We can hardly tell them to make an exception here."

"Oh well...yes, if they're adventurers..."

"We're well aware that the source of these items is unknown, but learning from mistakes is vital, so we allowed them to wear the pins. We find ourselves forced to view this state of affairs as part of an adventurer's ongoing education."

The other teachers nodded their agreement.

If this was how the school educational philosophy chose to handle the matter, the assembled moms could hardly argue with it.

"But that aside, we do have one serious concern," Mr. Burly added gravely. "If word spreads that the students have occupied the school... we fear the outcry could get out of hand."

No sooner than the words left his mouth than a pack of women turned the corner, heading up the road. All middle-aged, all dressed up, all looking incredibly stern.

The moment they saw the women approaching, a shudder ran through the faculty.

"O-oh, no! They're here!"

"They certainly seem quite worked up. Who do you think they are?"

"Those would be the students' guardians! Including the strictest parents, those most devoted to their children's educations—the PTA members! Ah, we're in trouble now!"

"An army of education mothers…I see. They all look like your type, Memama."

"How rude! I'm not like *them*. Mr. Burly, time to face the music."

"R-right…"

Mr. Burly abandoned his efforts to hide behind Mamako. Or rather, Medhimama bodily hauled him out in front of the crowd.

He bowed low, and the PTA formed ranks before him. At least twenty women, all staring daggers at him.

The mother at the front of the pack shot a momentary glance at the mom idols and frowned. But then her attention shifted back to Mr. Burly.

"Hello, Mr. Burly. I take it you're in charge? Let's get right down to business…"

"Y-yes! What brings you here today?"

"Ho-ho-ho! None of that, Mr. Burly. I hardly need to spell it out. I hear the students have occupied the school! Is this true?"

"I'm afraid so…I'm…at a loss for words. I could apologize, but…"

He lowered his head, unable to meet her eye.

Sensing weakness, the entire pack pounced!

"Apologies won't fix the problem! Will they, Mr. Burly?"

"If the teachers had maintained control, this would never have happened!"

"I-I'm aware of that…"

"We trusted you with our children and this is what happens?!"

"How could the school have raised our children into the kinds of thugs who would do such a thing?!"

"N-no, we haven't—"

"If this blemish on our children's records impacts their future, we'll hold you responsible! Do you have a plan to fix this?"

"This is caused by educational neglect! This is the faculty's fault! You admit it yourself, correct?!"

"Yes, I accept full responsibility. Our shortcomings..."

The verbal lashings of the PTA had left Mr. Burly in critical condition. His soul's HP gauge was rapidly dwindling and was now a candle in the wind.

The mom idols behind him shifted uncomfortably.

"I know how the guardians feel, but...this is hardly pleasant to watch," said Shirase-P.

"Yes...they should at least let Mr. Burly say his piece," agreed Mamako. "It's not like it was entirely thoughtless on his part."

"They need to calm down. Maybe if we spray water on them, they'll cool off."

Kazuno took out her tome, but...

"You should be ashamed of yourselves! Settle down this instant!"

A voice rang out, silencing the crowd.

Medhimama was striding toward the PTA, all eyes on her.

"You're all wailing like a pack of children! Have you no dignity at all? For shame!"

"Wh...someone dressed like you can hardly be lecturing us on shame or dignity!"

"Oh my! You take issue with my outfit? The nerve! These clothes were given to me by the Queen of Catharn! Do you wish to be jailed for lèse-majesté?"

"Er...the queen? *Those* clothes? Y-you're kidding, right?"

"It's the truth. Now..." Medhimama fixed her sights on the first mother to speak, the leader of the PTA pack. "I have a question for you. Have you heard about these pins that cause unnatural maturation in children? Answer me!"

"O-of course! Everyone knows. We've seen the reports."

"Then naturally you removed such pins from your own children."

"Well..." The leader had no response. Her eyes wandered, searching for a way out. "The school allows accessories, so...if anything happens, it's up to the school to..."

"I'm not asking about the school. You've come to the wrong shop to shift the blame, lady. I'm asking what actions you took as a mother. Go on, spit it out."

"Ack...I-I mean if the children grow up faster, their grades will improve! That's a good thing! I know they're dangerous, but I can't tell them not to wear something like that! That's how mothers think! You all agree, right?"

"Y-yes..."

"Our children's development matters more than anything..."

The mothers around her nodded, but none of them met Medhimama's eyes.

Medhimama sighed dramatically.

"You were perfectly aware of the problems with them, but you prioritized your children's grades and allowed it. And you call yourselves mothers. You're as foolish as I used to be," she said. A bitter murmur.

Medhimama turned her back, facing the closed gates.

"Mr. Burly. Are there any issues with the guardian of a graduate entering school grounds?"

"Er...? Uh, let me see. Generally speaking, only current students, teachers, and guardians of current students are allowed on the school grounds. So, guardians of former students would not be allowed, no."

"Oh? Then we'll just have to go in as idols."

"Huh? Idols? Idols...aren't specifically restricted, but...what?"

"Kazuno, these iron bars are in our way."

"Got it! *Bomba Sfera.*"

Kazuno shot an energy bomb, which struck the gates, causing a massive explosion. The iron bars and the gates were shattered into pieces.

They could now enter the school grounds!

"Oh dear...was that all right?"

"Not generally speaking, no," replied Shriase-P. "But Mom Idol Number Three is both detail-oriented and very forceful...let's call it characterization and approve."

"I'm honored by your praise. Come, everyone. Let's move."

With Medhimama in the lead, everyone headed through the remains of the gates.

"With parents like these, the children must be suffering. We must correct this mistake and restore their bonds. By first joining their classes! Ho-ho-ho!"

As the teachers and PTA posse stared in stunned horror, the mom idols commenced their assault.

Skirting depressions in the school yard, they made their way into the building.

It was quiet. No one in the halls, not a single sound to be heard.

"Since they've occupied the school, I expected more of an uproar..."

"But it's very relaxed. What a relief!"

"It appears there is no damage to the property. Since the teachers willingly vacated the premises, that sort of violence was avoided. A wise decision."

"Thank you. Praise from the former headmaster is most welcome. Gah-ha-ha!"

"Class is in progress. Silence!"

"Oh, right. Sorry."

Worried, Mr. Burly had chosen to accompany the mothers.

And...

"...Oh, you came along?"

"I-I am the guardian of a current student! I have the right to know what's going on with my child."

"Go ahead, suit yourself. But classes are in progress, so keep it down."

"I know! You are *so* spiteful! Humph."

Similar types rarely get along. Sparks flew between Medhimama and the head of the PTA pack, but the latter clearly wasn't planning to stand down.

Searching for the students, they found their way to a hall filled with ordinary classrooms.

Suddenly, the mother broke into a run, stopped outside a classroom door, and puffed herself up with pride.

"Medhimama, was it? I imagine you're unaware, so allow me to explain. This is the honors class! My daughter is a member. Ha!"

"Oh myyyy, is she? Well, let's see how she's doing."

"Go on! Observe how accomplished she is with your own eyes!"

Medhimama opened the door a crack, peering inside. "Squeeze in!" "No pushing!" The annoying mother did the same.

Inside, uniformed students were sitting at their desks, focused on their studies. The only sound was the scratching of their pencils.

"See? That one there! My daughter. Class president. Ho-ho-ho! When I heard they'd occupied the school, I couldn't believe it, but see? She's still studying. She's doing exactly what I say!"

"Yes. She certainly appears to be…but you're missing one thing."

"I am…?"

Medhimama could see the black cloud hovering over the students—the aura of dark power.

If you listened closely, you could hear them whispering:

"If I get better grades, I can skip a year and graduate early… Get results, graduate school, and leave home forever… Get away from my parents and live free…"

And not just the class president. All the students were whispering their desire to leave home, studying like they were possessed.

When the mother realized this, she gasped.

"Oh no…they're working this hard so they can leave us? That's why…?!"

"Perhaps she was originally very close to you. But the pins foster a desire for independence. Perhaps the reason they drove the teachers out was because they encouraged good relations with their parents. Either way…"

Medhimama grabbed the mother by the collar and pulled her away from the door.

Seeing Mamako's anxious look, Medhimama gave her a quick smile, then huddled up with the PTA mom.

"This is the result of your actions. What do you plan to do about it?"

"I…I just wanted her to grow up right. I never imagined that would mean she'd leave me…"

"Then we'll have to get rid of that creepy pin, and get her heart back at your side, where it belongs."

"But how? It's too late…"

"That's easy!"

Medhimama flung the door open and stepped into the class.

"Good morning, everyone! Mind if I interrupt your studies? …Come, Mamako, Kazuno! Hurry up!"

"Oh, right! Coming!"

"Er...uh, we're really doing this?"

"This is an idol's role! Of course we are. Line up!"

While the students gaped at them, the three moms lined up at the front of the class. This time Medhimama took the center, with Mamako and Kazuno flanking her.

One, two...

""""We're MOM-3, the all-mom idol group!"""""

Group pose: Nailed. The three of them were getting good at this!

The students were still staring in shock. The moms' grand entrance elicited neither cheers nor applause, but they paid no attention to *that*.

Subtly scoping out the pins on the boys' collars and the girls' scarves, Medhimama addressed the crowd.

"Assume that we are idols brought here to be teachers for a day! I have a question for you, students. Is this really want you want? Here you are, occupying the school, and you're just studying like you always do? How boring!"

"...But that's what's most important right now," the class president said. "Leave us to it! Weird people in weird clothes babbling about being mom idols have no right to interfere with my life plans."

This was the daughter of the mother in the hall, who was watching with bated breath along with Shirase-P and Mr. Burly.

But no matter how dead the eyes staring back at her, Medhimama responded with a smile.

"Studying is more important? But why is that important?"

"So we can be independent and contribute to society."

"Oh my! What a textbook answer. You think you can contribute to society and live a wonderful life just because you studied what school has to teach you? Heh. *Children.*"

"Wh-what's that supposed to mean? I didn't say anything wrong!"

"Oh, but you did."

These words were like a slap to the face, and her glare silenced the class president.

Medhimama turned around and wrote a single word on the chalkboard.

Play.

It was somewhat crooked. "Medhimama, *you* have bad handwriting?" "Shut up!" It wasn't *that* bad. And that wasn't the point here.

Dusting the chalk off her fingers, Medhimama turned back toward the students.

"School is a time both for learning and for play. You can't just study. So come on! Play! You've occupied the school! You can do whatever you want!"

"You can't just say that and expect us to..."

"My parents said I can play all I want once I grow up!"

"That's wrong. If you don't play as children, you won't learn how. If you don't know how to play, and how not to play too hard, then you'll make fatal errors as a grown-up. It's a very real danger."

"Well...yeah, I know some adults like that..."

"So while you still have a guardian to take responsibility, you need to cut loose! Not that we appreciate having to cover for your blunders, but, well...that's just another thing only parents get to experience. As a mother myself, that's how I look at it."

"I see...that does sound like an advantage."

The students were starting to get on board. It wasn't like they'd ever had anything against fun.

One after another, they stopped studying, their attention shifting to Medhimama. The noise level in the classroom rose until...

"Stop that right now!" the class president roared.

The room fell silent again.

But Medhimama stood her ground. Looking utterly confident. *Here it comes. Medhimama's trademark single-breath word torrent!*

"Oh? What are you yelling about? Sorrrry, I suppose you must not know how to play at all. Oh, dear, oh, dear. Such a shame. I should have known. If you're good at studying, *naturally* you have no idea how to even begin playing. You poor thing."

"Wha?! D-don't be ridiculous! I'm the class president! I'm the best at studying *and* playing!"

"Oh, don't try to force it, dear. You only think of a school as a place to study and have never even considered playing. Yes, a *complete* failure of initiative. If you don't know how to play, that's how you turn out. Poor thing. I *do* pity you."

"No, I...even at school...I play! At the festival or...the appropriate times! But that's only once a year and...I'm sure my mother would say to prioritize studying even then..."

"Oh? You want to be independent but you're doing what your mother says?"

"Th-that's not what—"

"Don't worry, I'm not making fun of you. I'm actually impressed! I have great hopes for you."

Medhimama had wound her up so much, she was clearly blurting out what she really felt. Even under the pin's influence, the girl's bond with her mother was still intact.

Medhimama pressed her advantage.

"Mr. Burly, if you could step inside for a moment."

"Y-yes! Coming!"

Mr. Burly hustled in. The students all braced themselves, but he waved one of his beefy hands to settle them.

"Mr. Burly, will you grant permission for a student festival? Oh, and permission for a MOM-3 live performance as well. You have the authority, yes?"

"A school festival...well, I suppose there is precedent for surprise festivals here..."

"Mr. Burly?"

Medhimama shot him a reproachful glare.

He suddenly got it.

"Oh no, I'm afraid that wouldn't do at all. We can't have a festival without the approval of the parents and guardians. Perhaps if the PTA members were all on board, or..."

"Oh my! Such a shame. Too bad."

Mamako and Kazuno had figured out what she and Mr. Burly were up to. All four of them looked at each other, waiting.

"Then allow me to grant permission!"

Shirase-P had pushed the class president's mother into the room.

The rest was up to her. Medhimama stepped aside, leaving the mother and Mr. Burly facing each other down.

"I think a school festival sounds like a grand idea! I'm entirely in favor of it. You have my approval! All these children work so hard, so why not make a special exception and let them play today?"

"I see...then...hmm...very well! Today we'll be holding a surprise festival!"

"Whaaa…M-Mr. Burly?! Mom?! You're sure?!"

"Of course! Your mom doesn't change her mind. For the rest of the day, play to your hearts' content! Come, hurry up and get this festival ready. Oh, but first, we mustn't get your uniforms dirty. Best to change into something you can move around in."

""""Yeah! Festivaaaal!""""

The boys cast off their jackets, and the girls their scarves. Expressions of pure joy spread across their faces…and the next moment, the pins fell to the floor with a clatter.

Seeing the problem resolved, the mom idol group gathered around a very proud Medhimama and clapped hands.

Time for the Gioco Accademia adventurer academy crown jewel—the surprise school festival!

Thanks to the technological power of the game world, decorations, displays, and shops alike were all pulled from existing data, and set up in less than an hour.

The starting gun signaled the festival opening, and the crowds flooded in. The depressions in the road leading to the school gates had filled in, and the crowd's progress was unimpeded.

Not just the crowd of overbearing, education-obsessed moms—every parent and guardian had been informed, and they were all here.

PARENT-CHILD PAIRS GET A SPECIAL BONUS!

These ads meant most students were exploring the festival with parents in tow. "Say ahhh!" "Stop that!" The boys looked slightly ashamed, but they *would*.

And the mom idols were observing the festival from behind the table set up on the event stage.

At least, those who had the spare time to observe.

"That was a pretty good stunt," Kazuno said, resting her chin on one hand as she watched the crowds.

"I thought it was lovely. Okay, all done! Thank you for supporting MOM-3, the mom idols! Hee-hee-hee!"

Mamako had been too busy with her hands to spare a glance at the festival.

"My class did a play at our high school festival. That was the last time I was onstage…actually pretty mortifying in hindsight."

Medhimama, like Kazuno, had nothing better to do than people watch.

The mom idols were holding an autograph event.

There was a long line of fans—in front of Mamako. Kazuno and Medhimama glanced at it and sighed.

"...The popularity balance in this group is totally lopsided. Makes us look bad."

"Mamako is already world-class famous. No point griping about it now, Kazuno."

"S-sorry...I don't want this to be a competition... There, all done! Thanks for your support! Hee-hee-hee."

"Don't worry about me. I'm only joking. I learned my lesson about trying to compete with you long ago. Still..."

"Having absolutely nobody ask for our autographs is still sad. I'd like to at least beat Kazuno!"

"I'm not about to let that happen! I'll—"

"If you don't mind?"

The class president's mother was standing in front of Medhimama. Her tone was as haughty as ever...but she bowed her head, and held out an autograph card.

"Oh my! That is a surprise. You want my autograph? Did my efforts earlier turn you into a fan?"

"Let's not get carried away. That's not it. You taught me a lesson, and as much as that vexes me, I wanted to get a word from you on paper. It can be a harsh rebuke or whatever you like. Just make it snappy."

"Oh? In that case..."

Medhimama picked up a pen and wrote:

Mothers should be as strict with themselves as they are with their children.

The size of the letters was all over the place, and the sentence went rather diagonal toward the end. "I knew it...!" "Shut up!" Medhimama had turned bright red.

Then she looked down at her own bad handwriting.

"I'm hardly a perfect mother myself. I'm always trying to be, but I never quite succeed. Consequently, I've had no end of setbacks raising my own daughter. I've made life quite hard for her."

"...So how did you change?"

"I apologized. And she was furious with me. After all the time I spent bossing her around and forcing her into stuff, how dare I try to fix it now? She had my number. But I felt I owed her that apology. Being strict with yourself means casting pride aside. If you really put your daughter's needs first, you have no choice."

"How's she doing now?"

"Our relationship is much improved. At least…I believe it is. Perhaps that's just wishful thinking on my part."

Medhimama smiled and held out the card.

The mother took it from her, looked it over, and turned to go.

"Honestly, I still can't bring myself to like you…but you've given me food for thought. I'll put this card somewhere I'm sure to see it daily, as a reminder to myself."

Her daughter had been waiting at a distance. She bowed, took her mother's arm, and they left.

And…

"Oh? Is this…?"

A glowing crystal appeared in front of Medhimama and was absorbed into her bosom.

Medhimama obtained the Parental Bond Tough Love!

"Oh dear…getting this just makes me want to see my daughter even more."

"Hee-hee-hee. Of course you do. You want to rush right to her side."

"Well, we solved the problem, and Memama got her quest item. Let's head to the next place. Also, I still haven't signed anything, and it's getting depressing."

Mamako had finally wrapped up the last of her line. Medhimama was looking terribly proud, and Kazuno extremely disgruntled.

"Then let's have you write in this, Kazuno," Shirase-P said, appearing beside her with a notebook.

"Don't sneak up on me like that! …Write what?"

"The lyrics to the song you're all going to sing! The school band helped out, and we've completed the music. Your concert is starting in five minutes, so do hurry."

"I've never written lyrics befo—wait, what? A concert? In five minutes?!"

"Come to think of it, I did ask Mr. Burly to approve our performance…"

"Memama! Why would you do that?! Five minutes to write a song we all have to sing?!"

"Well, we agreed to do it, so we're doing it. Be strict with yourself! That is my motto as a mother, and as a mom idol. Come, Kazuno! Make sure we're ready."

"Kazuno, Medhimama! This is our first concert! Let's make it a big success! Yay!"

"Even Mamako's into this?!" cried Kazuno.

Mamako had leaped to her feet and was now doing stretches to work out the stiffness from her marathon autograph session. She held her arms out in front of her...

And her Idol Sensor activated! Mamako knew at once where they needed to go next.

"This is...oh, dear! There's a war going on in Thermo!"

Everyone immediately tensed.

Following Mamako's memories, the group took a teleport spell to the town of Thermo.

The town entrance was flooded with people, all carrying a ton of luggage.

When the mom idols appeared, several glanced their way...but most were staring at the town landmark, the tower dungeon on the coast. They all looked anxious.

Piercing the very sky, the Solo-Killer Tower had plumes of smoke rising from the base. In the distance they could hear grunts and the clash of metal.

"Goodness! What a fuss! We'd better hurry!"

They pushed through the crowd and reached the coastal road. This gave them a better view of the situation.

A crowd of young adventurers, heavily armed, were racing across the bridge to Solo-Killer Tower Island.

Meanwhile, another group of adventurers were defending a barricade in front of the tower. They were holding their ground, but the fighting was fierce.

Kazuno and Medhimama frowned, examining the battlefield.

"They're really going at it! That tower is...?"

"If you reach the top, you can have any wish granted, yes? You all cleared it, right, Mamako? I remember seeing it in my daughter's progress reports."

"Yes, we did! You can't climb the tower without a lot of people, so we made a guild, gathered party members...oh, and this is where we first met Amante!"

"Mamako, this is no time to reminisce," said Shirase-P. She was watching the battle through a pair of binoculars. "The situation seems grim."

The army attacking the barricade wore pins with the kanji for *mom* written upside-down—the mark of Libere Rebellion, meaning these were the pins that accelerated growth in children.

The defense was being handled by a number of rough-looking adventurers and several mothers in full armom—armor versions of normal mom-wear.

The mom idols each took a turn with the binoculars, gasping.

"Oh dear! Those are the mom guild members! And their children!"

"The attackers all look like a bunch of kids, which means..."

"Terrible thoughts infected their minds, giving them violent desires. And Mamako's friends rose up to stop them. Then..."

"We have to back them up! Yay!"

"I dunno about 'Yay' but...how do we even get over there?"

The only way to the island was the bridge...which was absolutely packed with young adventurers.

Maybe a boat? But all the boats in the harbor had fallen into depressions in the water. There were none left in usable condition.

Kazuno thought for a moment, then pulled out her magic tome.

"Eh, worth a shot...*Grado Zero Assoluto!*"

She stood at the water's edge near the bridge, casting her spell toward the ocean surface. The ocean's dulled power had left the sea calm, with no waves at all—but now extreme cold blew over it, rapidly freezing the water.

And the frozen part moved straight ahead—forming an ice passage all the way to Solo-Killer Tower!

"Not bad. I mean...it'll be slippery."

"Well, we'll just have to be very careful! Let's go!"

"Wait, Mamako. You can't crab-walk across this thing—you're an idol! I suggest you use a sleigh. Much more elegant."

"Sleigh? But...where would we find..."

"I, Shirase-P, can info-P you that I have an idea. Leave it to me! Medhi-mama, hold this," she said, handing her the digital phonograph.

"Your ideas just fill me with dread...," Medhimama whispered.

Shirase-P stepped onto the ice.

She immediately slipped and fell. "Augh!" And cracked her head on the ice. Shirase-P was dead. Her body was soon inside a coffin.

The party obtained a coffin-shaped sleigh!

"This really does not sit right with me…but if we wasted Shirase-P's sacrifice, heaven only knows what she'd say to us later," said Medhimama. "Fine, everyone on board! Let's make a quick entrance."

"Then I'll turn that digital phonograph on!"

"And I'll rocket us over! *Bomba Vento!*"

A blast of wind, and the coffin sleigh swept the mom idols along.

All eyes on the bridge turned toward them.

"Mm? Yo, what the hell? Something's on the water!"

"Listen up, boys! …Uh, aren't we going *too* fast?!" said Medhimama.

"L-let's just introduce ourselves!" shouted Kazuno. "I'm Mom Idol Number—nope, too late…"

"MOM-3 will soon…aughhh…"

"…What was that?"

"……No clue."

The mom idols struck their group pose, but the Doppler effect made their words unintelligible, and they whooshed past the bridge in a blur.

They could soon see the battle for the tower with the naked eye.

Pocchi, the mohawk-sporting thug Mamako had reformed, was there with his mother. The two of them were standing side by side at the head of a mixed team of moms and thugs, desperately forcing back the onslaught of adventurers.

"C'mon, Pocchi! Don't be mean! Pull your punches!"

"I know! They're adventurers, too! They ain't gonna die that easy!"

"Wha?! Whoa!"

Pocchi grabbed a boy as he tried to climb the barricade, tore the pin off his chest, and threw both the adventurer and the pin into the ocean.

As he did, he saw a coffin with three passengers rocketing toward them.

"Mm? That…oh! Mamako! We've been expecting you! …Uh, that outfit is definitely unexpected, though…"

"Pocchi! Everyone! We're coming! One, two…"

"Hello! We're the mom idols!"

"MOM-3! Pleased to meet you."

The moment they reached the island, the mom idols jumped, landing safely on the ground! They nailed their group pose! Perfect mom idol arrival!

Behind them, the speeding coffin sleigh slammed into the tower wall. "I'll handle Shirase-P." "I'll resurrect her." Kazuno and Medhimama hustled over, leaving Mamako to race over to Pocchi's gang.

"It's been far too long! How have you been?"

"Great! Thanks. Masato's not with you?"

"Oh, it really is Mamako! You look extra fabulous today."

"Always so young! Makes me jealous. What's the secret to your youth?"

"I brought some tea and cookies! Let's have a little break and chat..."

"Yo, moms! This ain't no time for a chat! Remember what's going on here?!"

The moms had started converging like they were at a watercooler, not the front lines of a brutal battle. Magic attacks were thundering against the barricade, fire and shards of ice spitting through the gaps.

"Mamako, listen! I'll make it snappy! As you can see, Rebellion crews have gathered to wipe parents from the world! They must've heard the dungeon reward got reset! We're busy fending 'em off!"

"Got it! Then let us help!"

"No! Mamako, you hurry to the top! Given the situation...well, we figured you'd show up, so we cleared everything but the top floor! All you have to do is get up there and make that wish!"

"Er...we get to make the wish? Are you sure?"

"We considered wishing for a solution to this mess! But we don't really know what's going on! We figured it wouldn't be enough just to quell this conflict. But I bet you do!"

"Yes. The problem is much deeper than this one. We became idols to solve all such problems!"

"Then we'll let you handle it! Go on! ...Yo, Mom! Lead them to the warp floor."

"Right! Mom's got it! ...Come, Mamako! Shiraaase and the rest of your party, get moving! This way!"

"At the moment I am called Shirase-P—but perhaps this isn't the time. Let's go."

The mom idols and their producer/manager followed Pocchi's

mother to the tower doors. They paused outside, waiting for the tower to count them.

"Hey, wait! Damn! …Yo, mohawk! You're in the freakin' way! What the hell's wrong with you?! Only a lunatic would fight on the side of moms! You oughta be ashamed of yourself!"

"What's wrong with adventuring with your mom?! A snot-nosed kid who doesn't even know how to be grateful to his mom ain't got no right to mouth off to me! Rahhhhh!"

The rude adventurer was grabbed and thrown—and so was the adventurer behind him.

Smiling proudly at Pocchi's heroics, the five moms headed into the tower.

"Honestly, Mamako, you're the reason he talks like that… *Sniff.*" Pocchi's mom was tearing up.

"That's a boy you can be proud of! You can take him anywhere. Hee-hee-hee."

They raced through the tower halls.

When the reward reset, so did the interior layout—the rubble staircase was no more.

"This way!" They passed a flight of stairs, but they were ignoring the main route, headed for a little door in the back.

Inside the door was the warp room. Here, too, the tiles Amante had destroyed were repaired. Magic circles showed numbers from two to nine…

But some distance from them was another circle, glowing with a strange light.

"That takes you to Floor 99! The rest is in your hands, Mamako!"

"Got it! Let's go!"

Pocchi's mom waved them on, and they jumped in the circle—and were gone.

The mom idols reached the ninety-ninth floor. "Better save first." "There's no save system, though." It was certainly the place for saving your progress, but they elected to ignore Shirase-P's joke and climb the stairs.

Floor 100. Like a heavenly palace, a beautiful space surrounded by porcelain walls. No signs of the boss that guarded it—the final doors were flung open, and the staircase to the tower room stood before them.

Entranced by the solemn air, the party moved forward in silence. But as they reached the center, Mamako paused.

"Mamako? What's wrong?"

"Oh, just remembering what Ma-kun and the girls said here… They said they wanted to adventure with their moms! I was so happy, I couldn't stop myself from crying."

"I get that. And the other mothers and their children did, too, right? That boy…Pacchi, was it?"

"Pecchi. Didn't care for his face, but he had a rockin' bod."

"Neither. It's Pocchi," said Shirase-P. "And Kazuno, you really should look past a person's appearance to see the individual within."

"Hee-hee-hee…you sure do love muscles, Kazuno. Well, then…oh?"

Mamako was about to step forward…when a crystal glowing with a warm light appeared in the air in front of her and was soon absorbed into her bosom.

Mamako obtained the Parental Bond Making Up!

"That's right! Yes. This is my bond to Ma-kun. A warm, joyful treasure. Hee-hee-hee."

"And Mamako got her quest item, too! So…"

"Um, Shirase-P—we all have our Parental Bonds now. What do we do next?"

"No clue!" Shirase-P replied cheerily.

Kazuno and Medhimama both glared at her, but Shirase-P was not so easily perturbed.

"Ugh, this woman…," grumbled Kazuno. "*Sigh*, fine. I'm used to it by now."

"We've got bigger fish to fry," said Medhimama. "Let's take care of them first. Mamako?"

"Yes. Let's go."

They headed up the stairs to the roof.

As they climbed, Kazuno said, "I was thinking…if we make a wish to end the problems upending this world, and it's granted…does that mean we're done being idols?"

"Well…I suppose that would be mission complete."

"Then we'd all graduate together…?"

"Hmm…I guess so…"

Lost in thought, they climbed the rest of the stairs.

Before them stood a stone slab. The only words written on it?

MAKE THY WISH.

"I suppose the honor is yours, Mamako."

"Yes. We'll leave this one to you. Go ahead."

"Well, then…

Mamako stood before the stone slab.

Now for the wish!

"What should I say…? Um…"

"Repeat after me! 'Broadcast our song and dance to the whole world!' Go on!"

"Broadcast our song and dance to the whole world!"

""……What?"" Kazuno and Medhimama couldn't believe their ears.

"……Oh, my!" Even Mamako seemed surprised.

Shirase-P pumped her fist.

The stone slab sank into the floor, replaced by lights, mic stands, and what looked like TV cameras.

Shirase-P connected the digital phonograph to the sound booth. "I have always been a fast writer," she said, and quickly wrote up some lyrics on a set of cue cards. Preparations complete!

The stage was set for an idol concert!

"Heh-heh-heh. I knew this might happen, so I spent my time in the coffin thinking up the lyrics. Come, everyone! To the stage of our dreams!"

"Shirase-P! This was your goal all along?! You just had to force us into this?!"

"I've had all the crap I can take from you, woman!"

Kazuno and Medhimama both grabbed Shirase-P and shook her so hard, her neck looked ready to snap, but…

"Hee-hee-hee! Then we'll just have to do our best! Kazuno, Medhimama, and me! Three mothers brought together by our precious children!"

Mamako was already onstage, reaching her hands out toward the other two mom idols.

Holding Shirase-P in a Neck Hanging Tree, Kazuno and Medhimama glanced at each other…and couldn't stop themselves from smiling.

"……Okay, okay, fine. You talked me into it."

"After all we've been through, graduating without singing a single song would be pretty sad... Well, Shirase-P?"

"Absolutely. To restore bonds between parent and child and restore peace to the world...start the music!"

Freed from the mothers' clutches, Shirase-P flew into the sound booth and punched a button. Then she ran back out in front of the stage, holding up the cue cards.

This was the mom song.

"If you wanna laugh, laugh away! But be ready for the whip of love."

Dazzling beneath a rainbow of lights, Kazuno took a step forward with all the haughtiness of a gang leader.

"If I'm strict, it's because I'm thinking of you. After all..."

As imposing as she was elegant, Medhimama projected an intelligentsia vibe as she grabbed her mic.

And then Mamako spread both her hands.

"...I love you more than anything! Because I'm your mommy!"

Up-tempo music started blaring, and the all-mom idol group MOM-3's message song spread far and wide!

MOM-3's concert was broadcast to the entire world.

"Oh my! They certainly know when to go large, ho-ho-ho!" On the palace terrace, the queen smiled at the image projected in the sky above the Catharn capital.

The same image was playing in Maman Village.

"Oh! Mommy, look! Those old ladies!"

"Oh? What's going on? Huh? Huh? Huh?"

Their bonds restored, the little girl and her mother stared up at the sky. In the school town of Mahweh:

"Mother, won't you join me? One, two, MOM-3! MOM-3!"

"J-just this once! I'm not going to call myself a fan or anything!"

The class president and her mother mingled with the audience gathered at the school festival stage, waving glow sticks.

And far below the actual concert stage, at the base of Solo-Killer Tower:

"Uh, what?! Moms, singing and dancing? Wow! And they're super cute!"

"Plus, the one in the middle was the first person to conquer this tower. We sneakily made some commemorative goods in honor of her achievements, if you want some! There's a discount if you act now!"

"I'll take them at full price!"

The attacking adventurers threw the pin-studded equipment away of their own accord, replacing them with coats emblazoned with Mamako's face. Mothers good at sewing were busily working on Kazuno and Medhimama jackets, too.

The mom idol group's song and dance reached every corner of the world.

Children who had been unnaturally pried from their parents' sides found themselves pulled back. Mothers smiled again, and Mother Earth and Mother Ocean were restored.

"Dearest Mother Chaliele, I thought this would be the last we saw each other...but could I stay another night?"

"Stay as long as you want to. But Salite...do watch your step."

"Good idea."

Even in the elf village deep in the forest, a mother and a child clasped each other's hands, watching the depressions around them fill in.

"I don't want this pin!" "Neither do I!" "I like Mommy better!" "Mommy!" "Hugs!"

"Jeez, you finally snapped out of it? I was so worried! ...Still, this hardly seems fair. Those moms are having so much fun! They could have at least invited me! Heh-heh-heh."

Even in a world housed on a different server, a beastkin mother hugged her children tight, watching the sea restore itself as her brood jostled for position.

The song was for parents and children everywhere.

Which was why...

"...Nope, no matter how hard we look, we can't find a way."

"I figured there had to be a trick to it, but there *seriously* isn't..."

"Physical and magical attacks are equally useless. All they do is wear us out."

"I was sure there was a really big door here before! Awww..."

At Deathmother Castle, in the hall outside the throne room:

Masato and the girls had done a thorough search for the door that should have been there, but hours of investigating had gotten them nowhere. Masato, Wise, Medhi, and even the hardworking Porta had worn themselves out and were slumped against the wall.

But then...out of nowhere...they heard a song.

"Huh? That's...my mom's voice..."

"I think I hear mine, too."

"And I can hear Mama's voice!"

"My mom, Wise's mom, and Medhi's mom, singing together...? Sounds kinda like an idol song, too. That's giving me goose bumps—in a bad way... What's going on?"

Masato had no idea...but before the party knew it, their exhausted bodies were back on their feet, looking around, trying to locate the source of the song.

"Mm? Whoa, what the...?!" A crack opened on the wall behind them, and part of it crumbled away.

It left a hole just big enough for Porta to squeeze through.

"Um, the heck?" said Wise. "Does that, like, lead to the throne room?"

"I'll check it out! ...Hnggg...this doesn't go to the next room at all! It opens to a place I've never seen before!"

"The moment we heard our mothers singing, this happens... It feels a bit like there's a reason for that, huh?" said Medhi.

"Yeah...I feel like Mom...well, our moms...pulled one over on us again, but...moving forward definitely seems like the right thing to do. I bet this'll take us to Porta's mom."

"Then...Masato!" Porta looked up at him, earnest eyes gleaming.

Masato returned a reassuring nod.

Mom Roster Profile 4

Masumi Shirase

■Age:
I chose to cease aging once I hit twenty, so I can inform you that I remain twenty years old to this very day.

■Hobbies:
Making fun of high school boys—no, engaging in enjoyable interactions with other people's children.

■Specialties:
Failing to read the room, I suppose. I never mean any harm, but I'm often scolded for it.

■Best Feature:
"Your subtle expressions are so enchanting," is something I've always wanted to hear, even if that's asking a bit much.

■Childhood Dream:
I wanted to be popular, loved by anyone, able to make friends wherever I went. Alas, that proved to be nothing but a dream. Heh. Heh. Heh.

■Catchphrase:
"Results are everything." As long as it ends well, nothing else matters. My job is to lead things to that happy resolution.

■Child-Rearing Philosophy:
My daughter is still in kindergarten, so I'm trying to get her to do more things on her own, like cleaning her room and taking care of herself.

■To Your Beloved Child:
Mommy promises to come to your talent show next week. Mommy will be in the front row with a video camera, cheering you on. After that, we'll go out to a diner together.
　　Love, Mommy.

Chapter 5 Someone Who's Gentle, Free-Spirited, At Times Strict and Baffling. Such a Person Can Be a Weapon Sometimes.

They threw everything they had into their first song and dance. Their first performance.

When they were done, the three mom idols collapsed on the stage.

"Whew… Seems like we managed to pull it off somehow, huh?"

"Yes," agreed Mamako. "It was certainly amateurish, but I'm satisfied with our performance. I believe we've even accomplished our goal."

"That's right… I'm sure we have."

They closed their eyes, feeling the power of the restored Mother Earth and Mother Ocean.

If you listened closely, you could almost hear the cries of children and parents reunited the world over.

"Mamako, Kazuno, Medhimama, excellent work. That was a magnificent performance." *Clap, clap, clap, clap, clap, clap, clap, clap, clap, clap, clap, clap, clap, clap, clap, clap, clap, clap!*

"Okay, that's enough clapping."

"It's just spiteful at this point."

"I can info-P you that I am moved to the point of tears."

"Hee-hee-hee. That's just like you, Shirase-P!"

Shirase-P ceased her applause and approached the mom idols.

"Then let me be more sincere. Thank you, everyone. Your first concert was a success. Which means…"

"Finally, the moment we've all been waiting for!"

Mamako leaped to her feet, humming happily. Full of energy once more.

Kazuno and Medhimama glanced up at her, then grinned and scrambled to their feet as well.

"Yes. We've come so far and done so much."

"Can't exactly go home without dropping in on our kids. Well, Shirase-P? Any way to make that work? We'll take a 'probably.'"

"Very well, then Shirase-P will boldly make up a way for you to meet your—oh?"

Even as Shirase-P was proudly making no sense...

The crystals rose up from the mom idols' chests, glowing.

The light of the three Parental Bonds sketched out a door.

"Before I even had a chance to prattle any nonsense, your emotions caused a miracle! ...Let's go in."

The idols nodded at one another and placed their palms on the door.

With a gentle push, it swung open...and a strong, frigid wind blew out.

"So cold— Urgh...!"

"Hey! What the hell?! What's going on here?! Shirase-P just died instantly!"

"It's like it's rejecting us...but..."

"Ma-kun and the girls are inside... I can feel them! We have to go!"

With the snow slapping their cheeks, the mothers dragged Shirase-P's coffin after them, taking a strong step inside.

When the door closed, they found themselves in a white-out, unable to tell if they were outdoors or in. All they could see was driving snow.

They pressed onward and, in time, made out the faint outline of a castle in front of them.

"Oh? There's someone standing at the gate. That's..."

"Uh, Mamako? No..."

"Hahako, I believe. Exactly as she appeared in my daughter's progress reports. She really is exactly like you, Mamako."

They moved closer, their view clearing. Hahako stood before the snow-crusted castle, looking uncomfortable.

When the idols drew even closer, Hahako spoke.

"Thank you for that wonderful performance," she said. "As a token of my gratitude, I offer some information. Mothers are unable to proceed past this point. I'm afraid you'll have to turn back."

"Oh dear! That is a problem. There's no way in?"

"Inside this castle your children are desperately trying to accomplish something themselves, with their own power. I believe it is best to leave this matter to them. Sometimes parental interference just gets in the way. Do you agree?"

Hahako's argument made sense, but she seemed unsure of herself. She scanned their faces, awaiting their reaction.

The three mothers exchanged glances and smiled.

"Yes, you're right. That's why we're just here to watch. After all, we've come all this way! It can't hurt to look."

"...Huh?"

With a smile, Mamako had gone right past Hahako to the castle gate. "Oh?" And found an invisible wall. She pushed at it, but it didn't budge.

"Hahako, what's going on here?"

"Er, well...it's a sort of barrier. But...I'm not talking about whether it's okay to sneak a peek here. My point is that children grow even without parents..."

"I agree with that! But still..."

"That doesn't mean we should have no contact with them."

Kazuno and Medhimama joined Mamako at the invisible wall, feeling around it. "If magic would break this, I could do it..." "Would that work, though?" Perhaps it was better to exercise caution here.

Or...

"Um..."

"Oh, that's right, we've never met! I'm Mom Idol Number Two, Kazuno. Mother of that idiot Wise. This is Medhi's mother, Memama. 'Sup?"

"Could you not tell her your shortened version? My official name is Medhimama."

"Er, yes, I know who you both are..."

"Then in lieu of further introductions, let me teach you something. Mothers are selfish creatures. We want our children to grow, but we also want them to be children forever. And we struggle in vain to make both wishes come true."

"If you don't have that kind of nerve, you can never be a mother."

"You have to be honest with yourself. You want to see them! Nothing can stop you feeling that way. After all, they're your precious children! ...Oh, I know!"

Mamako touched her hands to her chest, manifesting the Parental Bond within. "I see!" "It's a distinct possibility." Kazuno and Medhimama followed Mamako's lead.

Light shone out from the three crystals. The invisible wall blocking their progress melted like thin ice, a hole yawning open in it.

The party could now enter Deathmother Castle!

"You're all...incredible mothers," Hahako said, shaking her head. Yet there was a hint of relief in her smile. "I'll put my faith in your words. And lend you a hand. I can tell you what your children know, what they're trying to do, and where they are now."

"Oh, that would be such a help! Please do."

"My idiot daughter's probably gonna get her magic sealed at least once..."

"Let us hope this is the only wall that gets knocked down."

"I see you know your daughters very well. Hee-hee."

Hahako led the way inside Deathmother Castle.

At that exact moment...

""""*Gasp...* They're coming?!"""""

A chill ran down three spines. Masato, Wise, and Medhi all froze in their tracks, their heads turning to look behind them.

But there was only the hole in the throne room wall they'd entered through.

Nothing else. No one was coming.

"I could swear I felt something super dangerous headed our way..."

"Y-yeah...I definitely got the same feeling... Guess it was my imagination?"

"I suppose. Let's hope so, at least."

"Then we press on!"

"Yeah. It'll be fine! Forward!"

The party began walking once more.

They had found themselves in a space filled with twinkling stars. A beautiful, desolate darkness.

Were those really stars? Masato squinted up at them, but...

"Hey, eyes forward. You're gonna fall."

"Oh, right. Yeah... Now's not the time."

They weren't round, like stars, but...like some sort of shining cubes? Either way, they were too far off to make out.

The only thing they could clearly see was the road in front of them, a narrow, winding path like the white line on a road. With Porta in the lead, they inched their way forward, like tightrope walkers.

"What *is* this place?" asked Wise.

"I dunno...but...there's a strange warmth to it."

"It's dark, but the darkness isn't absolute," said Medhi. "There's some light here, too…"

"Oh! There's something up ahead! I'll go check it out!"

Porta suddenly darted off down the path and bounded out into an open area. The others made their way after her.

The platform was about half the size of a soccer field, with a square stage at the center.

"Is this…a combat arena?"

"It kinda looks like one…which is weird."

At the four corners of the stage were statues of little girls and women, in pairs.

Each little girl had her hands out as if begging the women for something, but the women had their backs turned. It was unsettling.

"Masato, look at this!" Medhi called.

"What's up?" he said, running over. He noticed right away. "Yo, that's…"

The little girl had Porta's face.

And the woman's face looked exactly like the photo of Porta's mother from the wanted poster.

They ran around the stage, checking the other statues. All were the same.

"What does this mean? Why are there statues of Porta and her mom?"

"I think…we might be inside my mommy's heart," Porta said, staring forlornly up at the statue of herself. "Those stars are all photos of me. They're really far away, but my eyes can make them out. And these statues represent what my mommy and I are always like."

"…Oh."

"Whenever I try to talk to her, Mommy turns away and leaves, just like this. If I try to go after her, she runs…and gets farther and… sniff…farther away…"

"We get it. You don't need to say the rest."

Masato put his arms around Porta's head, pulling her close. He felt her nod against his chest and gave her head a good rub.

"But if that's the case, I have an idea. Just you wait."

Wise and Medhi had come running over, and he handed Porta off to them.

Masato went over to one of the mom statues, grabbed hold of the base…and turned! "Hngggg!" It spun 180 degrees until it was facing Porta's statue.

"How's that, Porta? Much better, yeah?"

"Y-yes! I like it that way! I'm very happy!"

"Right? Cool! Three more… Mm?"

But before he could head for the next target…

A strange object appeared between the two statues.

Something roundish, made of yarn all balled up.

"What the… Porta, can you appraise it?"

"Yes! …Hnggg…this…this, um, is part of something!"

"Part of what, though? Hmm…"

Masato decided to put the other three statue pairs the way they should be. Every time he turned the mother statue, an item appeared.

Each item was *something* made out of yarn. Something roundish. Something roundish with a vaguely earlike shape growing out of it. Two things like skinny arms. Two things like long legs.

"All the same kind of yarn, too," said Wise. "It's like someone's trying to knit a stuffed animal or something?"

"You're right. That's certainly a possibility," said Medhi. "…In a way, it's almost like someone was trying to make Piita."

"Oh, maybe they are! It's bigger than Piita, but the exact same color!"

"Hmm…"

Parts knitted together in imitation of the doll that hung from Porta's shoulder bag.

And they'd appeared the moment the parent-child statues faced each other, like they'd been waiting for that to happen.

Is this…a present for Porta?

Masato glanced up at the stars twinkling far above. Those stars were all photographs of Porta.

Were they really inside Porta's mother's heart?

It's certainly all about Porta, huh? This definitely…doesn't seem like hate.

For a moment, he felt hope.

But then…

"Whoa! M-Masato! The mommy statues!"

"Huh? …Hey! What the heck?!"

The four mothers were all turning on their own, back to their original positions.

And as they did, storm clouds swirled overhead. A huge, person-shaped thing appeared, headfirst, upside-down.

A demonic female form, covered in thorns from head to toe, screaming like a banshee.

"Eeeek?! Sh-she seems really mad! ...Is this because we took those items?"

"Maybe! But that ain't a reason to return them! Porta, you keep those pieces safe, and get to safety! We'll handle this!"

"Okay! Got it!"

Porta darted off to hide behind a statue. The thorn demon's eyes followed her.

"Nope, not her! Eyes over here!" Masato yelled, drawing his sword. He was about to attack...

No, wait. Is she... Ack!

That moment of hesitation made him switch targets, and his shock-wave struck the thorn demon's arm.

This was enough to turn her attention back to the center of the stage.

"Damn! That barely did anything!"

"I thought flying enemies were all yours?! Do your job!"

"You'd better not brag about being the hero chosen by the heavens *now*."

"No, that's not... I just wondered if this thing is Porta's mom, that's all! So I didn't use my full strength!"

Masato was starting to wonder if Wise and Medhi really had his back here.

But thorns were raining down on them too fast to ponder long. "Argh, she's fast!" Masato held out his left arm, deploying his shield wall. It only took a few hits before collapsing, but that got them through this volley.

And Wise took that opportunity to pull out her magic tome.

"Okay, this is my chance...!"

"You're going for it? Fine, go ahead! Don't blame me if it goes wrong!"

"You're seriously doing this with Porta watching?" said Medhi. "You're sure that's what you want?"

"Erk... If you put it that way...Medhi, she's all yours! You're good at this sort of thing!"

"Oh, I feel faint... I'm afraid I'll have to retire."

"Don't you dare run!"

"Right—Wise! Grab Medhi... No, crap, everybody ruuuuun!"

As they argued, a thorny hand descended toward them. Masato tried to warn them, but there was no way they'd make it in time.

He had only one option. "Both of you, duck!" ""Eep?!"" Masato grabbed Wise and Medhi, pushing them to the ground. Trying to at least keep the two of them unharmed.

Then he braced himself, ready to get skewered, his back exposed...

"Sheesh. What are you playing at?"

A shadow swept in too fast for the eye to see, unleashed a flurry of stabs, and deflected the trajectory of the thorn demon's hand.

As the giant hand stabbed the stage nearby, Amante made a beautiful landing.

"Why...are you...?"

"We said we'd show up at the perfect moment, right? Do me a favor and try to remember these things. I shouldn't have to explain everything."

"Besides, stopping to explain is just daaaangerous... *Spara la magia per mirare... Alto Forte! Ventooooo!*"

"Keep y'all's guard up! Mah!"

The thorns aimed at Amante were swept aside by a gust of wind, then punched away by a tiny fist.

With an athletic bound, Fratello landed next to Masato. Sorella drifted languidly by, riding her giant magic tome.

"Don't thank me, kid. You give us cookies, we bail y'all out. Simple."

"Cookies...?"

"Theeeese. You forgot them... Heeere!"

Sorella tossed a single box of cookies down to him—the ones Mamako had made as a greeting gift for Porta's mom, and that they'd carried through the first part of the castle.

"Oh, these! I left them behind? I didn't even notice!"

"Only one box? Weren't there two?" asked Wise. "...Oh, no, never mind. They ate one."

"Who eats a gift meant for someone else? No manners. Just raw gluttony," said Medhi.

"Sh-shut up! We got stuck rolling dice so long, we all got hungry!

But those cookies fully restored us...so thanks! But don't expect to hear me thank you for it!"

Mamako had chosen them at the store, so the cookies were clearly pretty good. "Porta, quick, over here." "Coming!" While the thorn hand was still stuck on the stage, Porta dashed over to them and put the precious box of cookies safely in her shoulder bag.

Then...

"Right, you owe us for bringing that to you, and you're gonna pay that debt by leaving this fight to us!"

"Huh? What do you...?"

"By the looks of it, this monster's not our Master herself, but clearly it has *some* connection to her. An expression of her heart? An upside-down demon...with thorny hands that can never hold what she really wants...whatever! It obviously has something to do with her."

"And that makes it ours," Fratello growled.

"Sooooo, you're in our waaaay. Piss oooooff. *Spara la magia per mirare... Alto Forte! Ventoooo!*"

"Uh, wait...?!"

The violent winds of Sorella's spell caught Masato's entire party. "Hey?!" "Eek!" "Whoaaa?!" They were sent flying off the stage, then off the platform it rested on...

Masato's party had been blown to the far end of this zone, completely out of sight.

"You knooooow, it just occurred to meeee...what if that coincidentally blows them right where they need to beee, and I accidentally really helped them oooout? That can't happen, riiiight?"

Or could it?

The three Heavenly Kings looked at each other, thought it over, and then snorted.

"Hell no! We wouldn't accidentally invite our enemies into the base and on top of that help them get right to their destination! That would be far too dumb!"

"Yeah, we ain't that stupid. Not a chance."

"Good, goooood. I meaaaan, we did take the mid-boss away from them, so I just woooondered...but naaah. Ah-ha-haahhh."

"Enough idiocy! Brace for combat!"

The thorn demon had finally freed its hand from the stage and was on the move again.

"We may have had our special skills stolen, leaving our combat abilities weakened...but we're gonna beat this thing anyway! Here goes!"

Amante put the full force of her physical skills into action, carrying Sorella on her shoulders and Fratello under one arm, darting about through the hail of thorns.

And she didn't miss the gap in the hail when it arrived.

"Fratello, now!"

"Mm."

Amante threw Fratello underhanded.

Fratello swung. Her bleary eyes locked on the face of the demon hanging out of the clouds above, and she rocketed forward, her fist slamming home.

Splat! **1 damage!**

"Mm. Without my skill, I ain't doing much damage! And that's just bad news."

"Hurry back here! I'll grab you again... Sorella, you're next! Bring in some undead!"

"Weeeell...this zone isn't really undead friendlyyy..."

"Use magic, then!"

"Sure, suuuure. *Spara la magia per mirare... Fusione Nebbiaaaa!*"

The magic tome opened above her head, and the spell activated. A powerful acid mist wrapped around the thorn demon's body, and the thorns visibly began to melt away. A horrible smell filled the air...

For a moment, the thorn demon's skin was smooth...but then the thorns began to regenerate.

"Those thorns make it hard to attack, but they heal so fast! What a pain in the ass! Still..."

"Go for it, Amanteeeee!"

"Get 'em, Amante."

"I'm going as hard as I can!"

The thorn fire rate was very fast. Even with Amante's fast footwork, it was all she could do to dodge. Mages like Sorella and Fighters like Fratello didn't have the speed to even try, so she was forced to carry them both.

Still she found openings to attack. "Go, Fratello!" "Mm." She threw Fratello at the thorn demon and caught her as she fell back. Time to dodge some more.

Then came Sorella's magic...

"I'm neeext...what should I tr—yeaghh?!"

"Sorella?! Argh, crap!"

A thorn in Amante's blind spot had pierced the magic tome above them.

And the tip of that thorn had reached Sorella's back, where she rested on Amante's shoulders.

"Th-that really huuuurts... This is your fault, Dumbanteeee!"

"Grin and bear it! Cast a healing spell or... Oh, right, you're offensive magic only so I'll do it! I'm a Magic Fencer! I can use basic healing—"

"This ain't no time to explain things, nitwit!"

"Er...augh...?!"

Distracted by Sorella's injury, Amante found herself about to be smacked by a thorny hand. Just before it hit...

Fratello kicked Amante to one side. "Fratello?" "Humph." Amante was flung clear of danger, but the thorny hand scored a direct hit on Fratello right in front of her.

Fratello was flung away, rolled to the edge of the stage...and did not get up.

"Now you've done it...not like we care about each other or anything...we don't...but I'm still mad!"

"Yeaaah...Amanteeee...go kick her aaaass!"

Sorella slid herself off Amante's shoulders, gave her a slap on the back like the rest was up to her, then collapsed onto the stage.

Gripping her rapier tight, fueled by the warmth on her back, Amante flew forward.

"This is totally not my thing, but I *am* gonna make you pay!"

She had to get a hit in. That was all she cared about—she made only the minimum necessary evasions, letting the hail of thorns glance off her sides, plunging headfirst toward the demon's face.

And Amante struck home, putting her full force into a blow directly between the demon's brows.

"How's that for... Augh?!"

A moment too late. Just before the rapier struck, a thorn shot out of the demon's brow, piercing Amante's shoulder. All she could feel was pain.

Amante lost her balance, and thorn-covered hands rushed toward her from both sides.

In a moment, she'd be swatted like a mosquito, and then it would all be over.

...Ugh, this sucks...

As she somersaulted through the air, her eyes focused on Fratello and Sorella, sprawled on the stage.

She had no intention of crying, but her vision blurred.

...Help...

But who would?

Masato's party? Or...

"If you're gonna just show up whenever...then now would be a great time...Hahako..."

"So you want my help?! Then you've got it! Hyah!"

"......Huh?"

As Amante was about to crash-land, something big and soft, like marshmallows, broke her fall.

Layer after layer of sprightly flowing water appeared around the thorn demon. A volley of water bullets began firing from all directions, and in no time the thorns and demon were riddled with holes—the demon had been vanquished.

"This space is filled with mom power! I was able to attack with all my might. Hee-hee-hee."

Hahako was standing in midair, a navy blue sword in her right hand, and Amante cradled in her left. She smiled.

"...Hahako?"

"Yes, that's right. At first I was just going to hide and watch. I didn't want to get in your way. But I just couldn't stand by any longer. I was so happy when you asked for my help! ...Oh, but we shouldn't be talking! I have to treat everyone's injuries!"

"R-right..."

"Medhimama! Can you cast a healing...? Oh, you already are!"

"......Uh, who the...?!"

Amante looked toward the stage, and saw a woman crouched next to Fratello, holding a staff over her.

She'd never seen this woman nor the one next to her (who had her arms folded arrogantly) but she recognized the woman who was

holding Sorella's hand and looking very worried. That, and the coffin lying behind her.

They were enemies. The same type as the awful people who had used and abandoned all of them.

But…they'd come running in when it really counted and offered help.

"Jeez…I will *never* understand mothers… And what are they *wearing*?"

This took the last of her strength. She grimaced.

And then Amante stopped fighting the warmth and comfort of the embrace, and slowly closed her eyes.

Meanwhile, the winds had flung Masato's party…somewhere.

"I bet they didn't mean to do this, but between explaining everything before we ask and accidentally sending us where we want to go, our enemies sure do make themselves useful… There we go."

Wise's levitation spell gently set the party down…

…in front of a massive door with the Libere Rebellion symbol inscribed on it.

"This is just like the door to the throne room!" cried Porta. "Same shape and size, exactly!"

"So what does that mean?" asked Wise. "What's this place we just crossed?"

"Some mysterious pocket dimension where your sense of direction or distance have no meaning," replied Medhi.

"Right. Anyway, I guess that means this door will take us to Porta's mom?"

They stood outside the door, taking a moment to catch their breath and calm themselves.

Masato put his hand on the hilt of his sword…and then released it.

"Porta, can you take out that box of cookies?"

"Yes! I'll get them right away!"

"Uh, Masato? Seriously? You're gonna roll in with a box of cookies and introduce yourself?"

"Of course, it's not like we *want* to fight, but…she may have other ideas. Between the monsters in the castle halls and that weird demon just now, I don't see this ending peacefully…"

"I know. But that's exactly why I want to play it this way. I mean,

Mom made sure we brought these cookies... I just thought that might be important, you know?"

"Huh..."

"Ohh...?"

"Wh-what? Spit it out."

Wise and Medhi looked at Masato, then at the cookies, then at Masato again. The both of them appeared legitimately impressed.

"You're actually doing what Mamako said without complaining!"

"I guess you've really matured. You're all grown up now, Masato! Heh-heh-heh."

"Sh-shut up! This isn't the time! ...Come on, let's do this."

"Yes! Let's go! One, two..."

Porta pushed the doors open.

As she did...

"*Trade-in,*" said a voice inside. The box of cookies flew out of Masato's hands.

And a 1 mum coin fell into his empty palm.

The box flew across the impeccably decorated room...to the hands of the woman on the throne.

"Oh...I meant to swipe the weapon you wield. What is the meaning of this?"

"I'd love to ask what you think you're doing but...for now I'll just be extremely glad I listened to my mom."

Wise and Medhi had both started to reach for their weapons, but they froze and retracted their hands.

Masato glanced at Porta, making sure. Porta nodded.

That's Porta's mom... No, right now she's definitely Dark-Mom Deathmother.

Armor. Rebellion coat. Haughtily perched on her throne like some sort of demon lord. Chin resting on her hand, looking everywhere but at them. Projecting arrogance in spades.

One eye on the monster-head-like shoulder bag floating above Dark-Mom Deathmother, Masato stepped into the throne room.

"Hello. We're Porta's party—"

"Masato, Wise, and Medhi. I appreciate you looking after my daughter."

"Hmm? Oh, so you know about us? And you're willing to greet us properly."

"I suppose she does think of herself as a mother on some level."

"......!"

Wise and Medhi's responses sent a little ripple of panic through Dark-Mom Deathmother...but she soon recovered and rose to her feet.

"Then let us begin."

"Huh? Begin what?"

"The battle, of course. You've come to defeat me."

"Wait, no, we—" Masato began.

"We came because I have something to tell you!"

Porta stepped forward, facing Dark-Mom Deathmother down.

Like she couldn't hold it back anymore—the emotions inside her were welling up, filling her eyes.

"I love you, Mommy!"

"Wh-what's this, all of a sudden...? Wait, that doesn't make sense. After all, I—"

"Maybe you hate me, but...even if you hate me, I still love you!"

"Wait, Porta," Masato said. He put a hand on her shoulder. "I don't think that's right."

Then he looked up at Dark-Mom Deathmother.

"Wh-what?"

"We just passed through a space that seemed like it was modeled after the inner workings of your heart. And seeing that, I thought... this woman doesn't hate Porta *at all*."

"That doesn't matter at—"

"It's the only thing that matters. I mean, the entire place was about your daughter."

"Yeah, that's right! Even the stars were all photos of Porta!"

"And every one of those photos was like a brilliant shining light! Like you'd taken the most precious memories you had and decorated your universe with them!"

"I don't know where you think you were, but I'm not listening to your nonsense any longer!" Dark-Mom Deathmother roared. "You are my enemies! We *must* fight! That's all there is to it!"

And with that, she raised a hand.

The mouth of the shoulder bag above her yawned open. Out came a crimson blade, a magic tome bound in chains, a bloody staff, a twisted bottle—a series of gnarly-looking weapons and items, which arranged themselves around the party.

"I'm a noncombatant, so your weapons can't harm me! But the forbidden items arranged around you ignore such restrictions, allow me to attack as much as I want! And I'll pay a good price for your equipment, so take it out and come at me!"

"No, wait. We're not here to fight you! We've got no reason to!"

"Oh, but you do! I'm the founder and leader of the Libere Rebellion! The greatest enemy you've ever faced! ...Isn't that right, Wise?"

"Hey, just because you gave my mom that weird power doesn't mean I'm holding that against you. That only happened because my mom is *very* dumb. And the upside of it all was...we got closer than ever before."

"Wha... Th-then, Medhi, what about you? You have all those dark, pent-up emotions! Surely you bear a grudge against me!"

"I'm actually rather grateful for what you did. There were certainly some bad things along the way, but in the end, I got to let it all out. And I finally have a good relationship with my mother."

"Spare me the honor-roll answer! Tell me how you really feel!"

"I just did! ...Although if I were to make one complaint...it's that you think I'm the type that would hold a grudge in the first place."

"Uh, you totally are, though... Whoops."

Medhi's smile never wavered. Still, she swung her staff sideways, and Masato dodged—"Gah!"—but it was a feint. The kick she aimed at his shin hit home. **Masato took damage!**

"Then Masato! I ask you, the hero! Those girls are not the only victims! Many other parents and children suffered at my hands! I brought chaos to the world! You must...!"

Sharp weapons clustered around Masato, as if challenging him to a fight.

Masato didn't even look at them.

"I ain't the kinda hero that beats the demon lord and saves the world, so I don't really care."

He started walking forward.

"You don't care...?!"

"Yeah, maybe this won't work. But that's okay. Doling out punishment is for the people who handle that stuff, like management or whoever. I'm just a normal hero, so... No, I'm me, and I'm here to settle the issue I care about."

"What...?"

"You're Porta's mother. How do you really feel about your daughter? Tell me that much. And be honest."

Porta stood next to him, looking very serious. Wise and Medhi followed; clearly, none of them were willing to back down.

Dark-Mom Deathmother refused to meet their gazes.

"...Fine. I'll tell you. This is how I feel."

She took a dark jewel out of her pocket and chanted:

"Monster Creation: Armed Ashura!"

The dangerous weapons surrounding the party were joined by a flood of shields and armor that came pouring out of the shoulder bag. Both the arms and the armaments clustered around Dark-Mom Deathmother.

The bits of armor came apart, forming a narrow torso and six floating arms.

Multiple shields formed the backs of the hands, and the fingers were blades and staves. The palms were covered in magical tomes.

A giant Armed Ashura made entirely of weapons loomed over them.

"Damn! She's hell-bent on a fight! ...Porta, get to safety!"

"R-right...I'll go hide!"

"You won't tell us how you really feel, huh?" Wise grumbled. "Instead you're gonna hole up and clamp your lips shut! That sure reminds me of *someone* we know!"

"I don't know who you could possibly mean," Medhi said. "...Anyway, here she comes!"

Six arms swung wildly, sharp points on a collision course with the party.

"Don't you dare! ...*Spara la magia per mirare... Alto Barriera!*"

Medhi's defensive spell activated. A sturdy dome enveloped them.

And a single poke from a finger easily pierced it, shattering the barrier.

"Wow... With just one hit...?!"

"Dodge! Now!"

From above and all sides, six sword-fingered hands were slicing toward them. Seeing Medhi stunned, Masato grabbed her, flinging himself sideways in the nick of time.

"Th-thanks! You saved me! This only sort of counts as sexual harassment!"

"I kept my hands in the safe zones, okay? Jeez, you can't *just* say thanks, can you?"

"You *both* need to quit goofing off!" Wise lightly kicked Masato and Medhi out of the way and opened her tome. "This is just a cluster of weapons and armor! All we've gotta do is blow 'em apart! ...*Spara la magia per mirare... Alto Bomba! Sfera!* And! *Alto Bomba! Sfera!*"

She chain cast, and two massive energy balls pulsing with explosive power let out a thunderous roar, spiraling toward their target...

And the target's hand spun, turning the back of the hand toward the spells.

When the spells hit that wall of shields, they didn't explode—instead, they vanished. They were absorbed completely.

"......Uh, really?"

"They can absorb magic? Then I guess I'll have to handle this! Flying enemies are miiiine!"

Masato attacked! Aiming at the same one Wise had, he swung Firmamento, the Holy Sword of the Heavens! A massive shockwave rocketed forward...

And another arm shot between him and his target, catching the shockwave on its set of shields. Masato's attack, too, was absorbed without causing any harm.

"Uhhhh...it can absorb physical attacks, too?"

"Absorbing all attacks is just absurdly hopeless... Argh!"

A hand came in to attack, and Medhi deflected it. A full swing of her staff, a powerful blow to the back of the hand...that didn't even make a sound. The impact was completely nullified.

"I'm afraid this *is* that worst-case scenario! All attacks are pointless!"

"But we can't *not* attack it! If we do nothing, they'll just hammer us!"

"Damn it! What do we do?!"

Each of the six arms was attacking wildly, constantly changing up the direction of its swing.

The party responded with shockwaves, fire and wind spells, bash damage, and instant death magic, but it was all taken in harmlessly...

And then they found themselves surrounded. The arms were spaced evenly, sixty degrees apart, palms facing inward.

"...Uh, this looks real bad."

"I agree. If they've been absorbing all our attacks and charging one of their own..."

"If it sucks in enough energy, then everything goes boom? I *really* hope that's not true..."

Each of the magic tomes forming the six palms was glowing. A magic circle with a six-pointed star embedded in it appeared around them.

It was happening.

"Argh, gimme a goddamn break! ...*Spara la magia per mirare... Alto Barriera!* And! *Alto Barriera!*"

"*Spara la magia per mirare... Alto Barriera!*"

"Hang in there, left arm!"

Three layers of magic barrier and Masato's shield wall. Just as they hit their full defensive potential...

The interior of the magic circle turned white. Energy fired from each of the six hands stacked, and the pressure and vibrations rocked the party.

All four barriers collapsed. They heard Porta scream.

The impact was like all their senses shattering...and then they dropped to the floor, like puppets whose strings had been cut.

"Ugh...damn...hey, Wise, Medhi...are you alive...?"

"...Not...sure. I might be...dead..."

"I-I'll heal us up... *Spara la magia...per mirare... Alto...Cura...*"

Forcing their aching bodies upright, they raised their weapons once more.

The magic circle dispersed; the six arms were flying all over the place again, like they were waiting for the party to attack.

"Thanks, Medhi. You really saved us."

"It's not often I really get to act like a healer, but I can't say I'm all that happy about it."

"You know things are bad when the healer's laid out flat, too. Damn. So...Masato? Any ideas?"

"Uhh...we really gotta do something about these shields, but..."

"Yeah...y'know, it ain't like all six sets can absorb all types of attacks."

"I noticed that. When Masato tried to attack the one that absorbed my spell, another one came in to defend it. Which means..."

"If we can figure out which one can't absorb the attack, and hit it with the right kind of damage...but how do we tell them apart?"

The six arms looked exactly the same. There was no obvious difference in the weapons and armor they were made of—colors, shapes, and positioning were all functionally identical.

Only way to find out is to attack...

Well aware this would only charge the enemy's next attack, Masato decided to start with the nearest arm...

"Wait!" Porta cried. "That one absorbs physical damage! Those shields are weak to magic!"

Masato cut the attack off, but kept his sword pointed at the target.

"Wise! Hit that one! Don't miss!"

"Okay, I got this! Finally! ...*Spara la magia per mirare... Alto Bomba Sfera!*"

A magical energy blast shot toward the arm Masato had targeted.

Another arm tried to step in. "Nope!" Medhi jumped in front of it, knocking it aside with her staff.

Wise's spell hit the target. There was a huge explosion. The armor and weapons remained intact but scattered everywhere.

Medhi had been right next to the explosions and one of the shields smacked her in the head, "Ow!" but the damage was minimal. It did leave a bump, though.

"Wise, did you do that deliberately...?" she growled.

"No, no, no, no! I'm not *that* competent!"

"Either way, nice teamwork! And the MVP is..."

Masato spun around and looked straight to where Porta was hiding, by the big door.

"Masato! Should I...?"

"Of course! You're the key to this whole fight, Porta! ...We'll take care of these arm things, and then make your mom tell us how she feels!"

"Okay! I'll do my best! I'm going to really really try extra hard so Mommy will tell me her feelings!"

"Yeah! That's the spirit! You're in charge here!"

They were fighting clusters of armor and weapons. Porta's Appraise skill could easily tell what traits each had.

Five arms left. They were circling the party rapidly, as if fearing appraisal.

"Tch...they're fast... We need to slow them down somehow..."

"Leave it to me! I can stop them!"

"Y-you can...?"

Porta pulled a bottle out of her shoulder bag, then unhooked Piita and poured the glittering fluid into Piita's mouth.

The doll immediately started getting larger. Once it had reached full size, Pretty Prodigious Piita toppled toward the circling arms.

Two arms failed to get away in time and were both pinned down with the shield side exposed.

"Nice! Then I'll attack…"

"Wait! They'll both absorb your shockwaves!"

"Huh? Oh, then, uh…go ahead…"

"The one under Piita's face is weak to water and ice! The one under Piita's belly is weak to bash damage!"

"Got it! …*Spara la magia per mirare… Alto Ghiaccio Grumo!*"

"I'll take the other one! Rah!"

A massive hailstone appeared above the party and fell toward the shields that were weak to ice, crushing them. Meanwhile, Medhi's staff bashed the other hand to pieces. Both arms under Piita were demolished.

"R-right! Three left! Halfway there! I'll handle the—"

"Wise, the two near you are both weak to fire! Medhi, the one near you has no resistance to death spells!"

"Fire?! I'll take them both down! …*Spara la magia per mirare… Forte Fiamma!* And! *Forte Fiamma!*"

"I'll send you to meet your maker! …*Spara la magia per mirare… Morte!*"

"Uh, hey…"

Two of the remaining arms were enveloped in searing flames, crashed to the ground, and were gone.

The last one gave the reaper a bit of a chase, but finally fell apart in the air.

All six arms were defeated!

"You're *too* good, Porta! Perfect instructions! You made it so easy!"

"And the way you enlarged Piita to trap those two was really clever. Porta, I think you might be a good fit for shot caller."

"Th-thanks… Eh-heh-heh…" Porta looked embarrassed. It was adorable.

She shrank Piita back down and hooked it on her bag again.

Porta's smile sure was cute, but… "…Mm, fine, whatever." …Masato had trouble seeing her through his tears.

He'd done so little, he might as well not have been there, but…at least the battle was over.

"…Huh? Whoa!" yelped Porta. "Careful! It looks like we're not done yet!"

The armor and weapons around them started clattering.

One by one they rose into the air, clustering together again.

"Hey! Masato...no, great leader Porta!"

"Masa—I mean, Porta! What's going on here?"

"Okay, you *both* did that deliberately... But I'll have to gripe about that later, huh?"

"Um, um..." Porta said, peering close. "Oh! I think that's the cause!"

She pointed at the chest made of bits of armor. There was a dark light shining through the gaps.

"So the dark jewel is the core, and moving the whole shebang? In that case..."

"Porta—just kidding, Masato!"

"Porta! Ha-ha, no, Masato!"

"Masato! This one's yours!"

"Yeah, yeah, everyone loves Port—wait, me?! Now?!"

He couldn't even see the jewel itself. The gaps in the armor weren't even wide enough for a sword to enter—but he had to get an attack in through them somehow.

"C'mon, Masato! Show us what you can do! ...*Spara la magia per mirare... Colpire!* And! *Colpire!*"

"We believe in you! ...*Spara la magia per mirare... Colpire!*"

"You're just *thrilled* to foist this problem off on me, huh?"

Wise and Medhi tacked on the pressure along with a spell that buffed his accuracy. Masato raised his sword.

Porta's face was right next to him, beaming with trust.

I know! I've gotta do this.

Faith can move mountains. And this mountain had plenty of holes.

He was facing a mother hiding the emotions she needed to express to her child who needed to hear them.

"Sorry, I'm gonna be a little blunt. Porta's asking for love with all the purity and sincerity you could ever hope for. How can you not respond?! Get the hell out of there and talk! You're her freakin' mom!"

He put his back into a mighty swing and fired the narrowest, sharpest shockwave he could.

It shot directly into the chest of the Armed Ashura.

It had been trying to regenerate its arms, but instead...it fell limply to the ground, its torso armor scattering.

And standing below the shattered fragments of the dark jewel was Dark-Mom Deathmother.

She stared at her feet, looking utterly spent.

*　　*　　*

When Dark-Mom Deathmother said nothing, the party was left exchanging glances.

The only answer they found was to move close enough for her to see, confronting her face-to-face.

"Porta, let's go."

"Okay!"

Masato took Porta's hand. Wise and Medhi followed right behind.

"Tell her how you feel. Your honest emotions. What do you really think of Porta?"

The hovering weapons and armor all came rushing toward them.

But the moment before they hit, they changed directions, just barely missing.

She really isn't the kind of person who can hurt someone...

He was sure Dark-Mom Deathmother was actually nice.

Then her eyes stopped avoiding them. They shifted, locking on to her daughter.

There was no trace of hatred in those eyes.

I knew she didn't hate her. There must be a reason why she acts so distant.

If they could just do something about that, then Masato was sure Porta and her mother could make things work.

Which was why they had to press the point, even without knowing the reason.

"Stop it! This is all too painful!"

The words erupted out of her.

Dark-Mom Deathmother covered her face with both hands, sinking to her knees.

"My honest emotions?! What do I think of my daughter? That's... obvious...!"

Her eyes turned to the ceiling.

"I love her! I love her more than anything!!"

A cry from the heart.

The words they'd wanted to hear, but the pain behind them froze everyone in their tracks.

"Mommy...you love me...?"

"If you love her, then..."

"But I can never tell her that! I can never show that! There so much I want to do for her, so much time I want to spend with her, but I can't! Not ever!"

"Wh-whoa, calm down here..."

"I don't have the time! I'm too busy! Work work work work! I have to work to live so that my daughter never wants for anything! Part-time, contract work, salaried...I worked my ass off climbing the ranks! And each step left me with even less time! I couldn't do anything about it!"

"Please, settle down! Relax!"

"And now this?! A game where you get to adventure with your mother?! Where you get to fix problems in parent-child relationships? When all they need to do is spend some time together?! It's insane! And I'm too busy managing *these* people's problems to see my own daughter today, tomorrow, or any other day! ...Why can't these people understand that just being together is all it takes to be happy?!"

Dark-Mom Deathmother hung her head, then stood up.

"That's why...at first, I was just lashing out. I was jealous of the other parents. I was frustrated... Depressed... I just wanted to destroy everything. But my plans failed. As much as I hated myself for it, I just wanted to take all these other moms down with me, make a world where it was only natural not to have your mom around, one where children could happily live on their own... But Mamako and those other mothers ruined that, too. I can't do anything right! I'm a total failure! So go ahead, heroes. End me!"

"Like I said, we're not here for that!"

"No, you must! Useless mothers like me should be eliminated."

"We can't do that! You're Porta's mom!"

"And you do still care about her! You're not someone who needs to be defeated. Get it together, for her sake!"

"My daughter will be fine. She's got you three. You're better parents than I ever was. You've done far more for her than I ever did. She's better off without a hopeless failure like me. Yes. She should live as far away from me as she can."

"Is that why you were so hostile? Always pushing her away? Even though you adore her? Jeez. What a mess. There are so many other things you could have done!"

"Maybe so. But I couldn't think of any. I didn't have time to think! All I ever had was the bare minimum of maternal feelings…and the fear that my daughter would be ruined if someone like me raised her. That's why…"

A sad smile played across Dark-Mom Deathmother's lips, and then a small bottle containing a dangerous-looking liquid flew to her hand.

"…I leave my beloved daughter to her wonderful party…and this foolish mother takes her leave. Look after her for me."

"No! Mommy!"

But even with Porta's eyes staring up at her, Dark-Mom Death-mother downed the bottle.

A trail of blood ran down her lips, and her body crumpled to the ground

"W-wait… What did she just drink?!"

"Poison! W-we have to get her an antidote! Mommy! Mommy!!"

Porta frantically pulled out a medicine bottle and tried to run to her.

But the floating weapons and armor blocked her path. "Let me through! Ow!" When Porta tried to push past, a cut opened on her hand. Normally, even if a noncombatant like Porta were attacked, nothing could harm her—but these were all forbidden items.

Porta kept pushing forward, and the weapons just kept cutting her.

"Porta! Don't! We'll open the way! Wise, Medhi, come on!"

"Obviously… Yikes! Hold up!"

The moment Wise opened her tome, a chain-wrapped tome flew out. Its pages opened, and a magic energy bomb shot out. "That's *Bomba Sfera*…!" It hit Wise hard, blowing her away.

"It insta-cast the moment it opened?! How is that fair?! …Medhi! Cure Wise!"

"S-sorry…I'm in a bit of trouble myself… Argh!"

The bloodstained staff was floating over Medhi's head, raining curses down on her. Bind effects were appearing all over her body as she was struggling to free herself, already on her knees.

"Seriously? Another super dangerous weapon? Hang on—I'll knock it down!"

"No, wait! Masato! Careful…above you…"

"Huh?"

He looked up just in time to see the crimson blade slicing down right toward his head. "Gah!" He managed to raise his Holy Sword in time to catch it, but it was a heavy blow. Masato was now pinned to the spot, too.

"It's too much! I can't afford to get stuck here! I need to do something soon, or..."

Dark-Mom Deathmother was writhing around in pain, but her movements were quickly growing feeble.

Porta had the antidote, but the flurry of weapons and armor was pushing her back, not letting her get close.

Wise was hit with another spell, sinking into a cloud of smoke. Medhi was too tightly bound to move at all.

"We gotta do something... Damn it... If only Mom were here!" Masato cried. The only thing he could do was think of the person he trusted most.

But then...

"And that's our cue! Start the music! Go, MOM-3!"

"......Huh?"

Shirase-P had popped her face out from behind the giant door behind them. She flipped the switch on the digital phonograph and an up-tempo pop song blared. A total mismatch for the present situation.

"Being strict is an expression of love! With my daughter close by my side, together we'll strive for greater heights! I'm Mom Idol Number Three—Medhi's mother, Medhimama!"

"Neither of us are honest with our feelings! You gotta problem with me, spit it out! Family squabbles are my thing! I'm Mom Idol Number Two—Genya's mama, Kazuno!"

"My love is boundless! I love you sooo much, Ma-kun! Let me give you a biiig hug! I'm Mom Idol Number One—Ma-kun's mommy, Mamako! Hee-hee-hee!"

All together now!

""""The all-mom idol group MOM-3 is here!""""

They nailed their group pose!

Their real moms, wearing idol costumes, striking an idol pose!

""""...Blergh...""""

The effects of the sudden mom arrival skill, A Mother's Visit, made Masato, Wise, and Medhi's eyes roll up in their heads, and collapse in a shower of blood.

But then another mom idol skill activated!

"Let's begin the Pat Pat Event!"

"Ahem. The mom idols will now be dispensing free head pats to anyone with a Pat Pat Ticket. Anyone who wants a ticket, please line up! Quantities are limited, so do hurry."

Exactly like those Handshake Events that let you shake an idol's hand—only with head pats.

In response to this call, the weapons stopped menacing Masato and the girls, no longer blocking Porta's path. Instead, they flocked over to Shirase-P, fighting one another.

Their path was open!

"Porta, go! Hurry!"

"Y-yes! …Mommy!!"

Clutching the antidote, she ran to Dark-Mom Deathmother's side.

When Porta's mother's eyes fluttered open, she saw Mamako smiling.

"…I knew you'd do it… You always show up, show off what happy families are like, and put a stop to all my plans… What a family…"

"We're a normal hero, and a normal hero's mother. Hee-hee-hee."

"Nothing normal about you… Ugh…fine. Losing so thoroughly actually makes me feel a little better. All that envy and frustration…I'm just past caring."

"I don't think being a family is about winning or losing. But if you're feeling better, I'm glad. Can you sit up?"

Mamako put an arm around her back and got Dark-Mom Deathmother upright.

There was a noise nearby, and she turned to look…and saw Kazuno and Medhimama stuffing weapons and armor into Dark-Mom Deathmother's shoulder bag. When they were done, they pulled the drawstring tight.

Porta was in front of her. On her knees, covered in cuts, trying very hard not to hug her but reaching the end of her endurance and leaning closer.

Avoiding Porta's eyes, Dark-Mom Deathmother hung her head.

"Why did you save me…? After all I've done, you must hate me."

"I don't hate you! I love you, Mommy!"

"Don't be silly. Why would you? I've never done anything for you...
Quite the opposite. I've pushed you away at every turn."

"I don't care! You said you love me, Mommy! That's all that matters!"

"It is...?"

"Oh, for cryin' out loud! You both love each other, so what else could
possibly matter?!"

"There's nothing more pointless than searching for concrete reasons
for loving someone."

Done cleaning up, Kazuno and Medhimama came toward them,
shaking their heads.

Mamako smiled, and then gave Dark-Mom Deathmother a pat on
the back.

"Deathmother...no, Ms. Hotta. You're a very dedicated woman. And
I think you treated your child less as a mother than as a grown-up, as a
hardworking member of society."

"Meaning...?"

"Y'know, like a sense of duty, a fair trade, that sort of thing," said
Kazuno.

"You certainly never expected anything unconditional," added
Medhimama. "You've been so heavily involved in what lies between
parent and child, between those two opposing forces, that your own
parental nature remained stunted."

"Stunted? Then...what was I supposed to...? How can I accept my
child's feelings the way a parent would?"

"That mindset is already a mistake."

"Looks like we have a long way ahead of us."

"We'd better start training now!" Mamako said, flexing her arm.
Then she smiled. "Children grow up even without their parents, but
parents can't grow without their children. So we'll have Porta raise
her! ...Are you ready, Porta?"

"I am! I'll raise my mommy!"

"Huh...?"

Her beloved mommy was still hesitant, but Porta just dove on in.

Then she pulled four items from her shoulder bag—the misshapen
knitted pieces.

"I found these inside your heart! Do you recognize them, Mommy?"

"Y-yes...those are the parts of the knitted doll I made. Since I couldn't accompany you inside the game, I wanted you to have something besides the safety alarm, so I tried making this…but I just didn't have time to finish it, so the pieces were in my desk drawer. But why are they here?"

"I don't know! But in that case, then I know what to do! …I'm going to ask you to finish this and give it to me as a present!"

"W-wait—if you want a present, I can buy you something much better! I'm not so good at this sort of thing… I know it's not going to turn out well…"

"I don't want anything else! This is what I want! If you make this and give it to me, I'll love you even more!"

"…Is that how it works?"

"It is! Please!"

"O-okay. Then…"

She no longer seemed like a demon lord. Dark-Mom Deathmother was gone. Saori Hotta's face was that of a mother doting on her beloved child. She took the knitted pieces.

And her gaze turned directly to Porta.

"Before I make this, can I ask you for something?"

"Sure! What is it?"

"You can say no if you want. But…can I give you a really big hug?"

"Of course!"

Porta threw herself into her mother's arms, looking utterly content.

Saori caught her and looked down at the child in her arms as if her life was now complete.

Mamako was tearing up a bit, and Kazuno and Medhimama stood by her side. Everyone smiled.

And a little farther behind them…

"Well, the damages were significant, but all's well that ends well," Shirase-P said, glancing only briefly at the children lying unconscious on the ground nearby.

Mom Roster Profile 5

Hahako

■Age:
My data is set to the same age as Mamako, but it's been less than a year since my initial creation.

■Hobbies:
Gathering data on mothers. There are many different types of mothers, and this proves very informative.

■Specialties:
I can instantly pinpoint my children's locations. Well, more accurately, the locations of my potential children.

■Best Feature:
I would love it if someone found my motherly qualities appealing.

■Childhood Dream:
I didn't have a childhood, so this is a difficult question... But had I possessed a child form, I think I would've dreamed about being a mother one day.

■Catchphrase:
"Family," of course. I wish to be part of one someday. That's my goal.

■Child-Rearing Philosophy:
How should a parent handle their children? It's a rather complicated concept... I hope there's something we can do together to become a happy family.

■To Your Beloved Child:
You might not like it, but in my heart, you three are already my children.
　I don't claim to know everything about being a family or the nature of love, but I do know one thing for sure—
I want to give you all a big hug.

Epilogue

The scream was so loud, it nearly shattered the windows in the Mom Shop.

"Have you lost your mind, Mom?! I mean, you've *always* been crazy, but this is going too far! Showing up in an idol costume? Are you trying to *murder* me?!"

"Oh, whatever, Genya. I looked good. I had my qualms at first, but you get used to it. You should try it on! I'm happy to loan it... Oh, no, wait, my boobs are so much larger, it would never fit you. Pfft."

"Ah, I see, you want some of this then?! Put 'em up!"

"You're on! This is how we talk things out in our family!"

Wise and Kazuno began grappling. Lots of boob grabs involved. At least take it outside! But no, they were rolling around the Mom Shop floor, causing a huge scene.

Meanwhile...

"M-Medhi, would you like some more tea? It's very good."

"...It is. I'd be delighted." ...*Rumble*...

"S-so, like I said, that was work! Our idol activities helped save the world! Dropping in on you was merely a side benefit. The whole thing was requested by the queen herself, so I could hardly turn her down, could I? Of course I couldn't. So..."

"...Mother, don't you think it's time you left?" ...*Rumble*...

"My stay here isn't up yet! Medhi, please! Calm yourself! Don't look at me with such darkness in your eyes!"

There was a powerful menacing aura on one side of the table. Medhi had become one with the darkness inside her, and Medhimama was desperately holding her ground—but clearly in grave peril.

Another table was an oasis of peace, heedless of the chaos around them.

"You hook the yarn with the needle and turn it...like this?"

"Yes! You twist it, and then go here, and twist again!"

"Twist...? Oh, it came off! This is so hard... It would be so much faster if you made it, Moko. Just use your Item Creation and—"

"No! I won't accept it unless you make it yourself, Mommy!"

"O-okay, I hear you. I suppose this is a mother's trial. I'll do my best."

"Yes! I'll cheer you on!"

Saori was struggling with her knitting, but Porta was clinging to her side, and they were finally spending time together.

Literally clinging—Porta's cheek never left Saori's arm.

"That looks like it'd make it hard to knit..."

"Hee-hee-hee. It does, but that's lovely, too."

"Pointing it out would just ruin it."

"Yes. We'll have to restrain ourselves."

Masato, Mamako, and Shiraaase were watching the other families from the counter. "Here you go!" Mone set teacups in front of each and told them to help themselves to anything else they needed.

"So Porta's real name is Moko?"

"Isn't that an adorable name? Perfect for her!"

"Names these days are so weird... Makes me feel old..."

"You're far too young to talk like that, Masato. But I suppose I'd better summarize things," Shiraaase said, straightening up. She gave Masato a long look...and then turned her head, bowing to Mamako. "Mamako, you've done it again! You've stopped the unnatural child development, restored both land and sea, and reformed Hotta, the leader of the Libere Rebellion! And left the children utterly astounded once again! A complete triumph!"

"The queen sent a letter thanking you, too! That's amazing," said Mone.

"Yeah, yeah, I get it. Once again, Mom—well, the mom idol group—totally overshadowed us."

"I don't think we did! Ma-kun, you accomplished so much. I'm very impressed by how much you've all grown."

"This is true. When you were in dire straits with no way out, you had the courage to yell, 'If only my beloved mother were here!' In that instant, I knew you had truly matured. Magnificent."

"Now you're just putting words in my mouth! I didn't yell all of that! I..."

Masato glanced over, saw how happy Porta and Saori were, and smiled.

"…I just took a cue from Porta and figured it wouldn't be too bad to rely on her now and then. That's all."

"Hee-hee-hee. You can rely on Mommy anytime! Or…that's what I'd like to say, but…"

"But what?"

"Mommy's been thinking it might be better for you if I stopped holding on to you so tight."

Mamako frowned, wrestling with this thought. She gave Masato a long, searching look. "But maybe not just yet." "Hey!" She put her arm around his, pulling him against herself. Squeezing tight. Looking very happy.

"We must be extremely careful how we go about letting you be more independent, Masato. Imagine what would happen if Mamako became seriously depressed…"

"I doubt it would end with a few dents in the ground and ocean," Mone growled.

"Holy crap?! Yeah, I don't want our relationship to literally destroy the world!"

"We can't rule out that possibility…but before the world ends, I have some paperwork!"

Shiraaase stopped fanning his fears and flashed a businesslike smile. She pulled out several documents, running her eyes over them.

"First, as for Hotta's punishment, much like Wise and Medhi's mothers, we've managed to tip the scale in her favor. Given the gravity of the incidents and the fact that Hotta was part of our organization, she's going to have to attend a *lot* of hearings and write a mountain of apologies. But we plan to let her take her time with those, prioritizing time spent with her daughter."

"I extend my gratitude to management's generosity."

"As for the Libere Rebellion that Hotta founded, we've discovered a number of system engineers involved in the data tampering, but they were all merely following Hotta's instructions, so with their leader out of commission, their actions have followed suit."

"That means all problems in the game world are over! That's lovely."

"Precisely…is what I'd like to say, but there is one problem remaining."

"There is? What's that?"

"The Rebellion's core members, Amante, Sorella, and Fratello. All three remain at large. With the Rebellion itself destroyed, we have no idea what they'll do next..."

"Uh, but they're right over there?" Mone said, pointing.

""""What?!""""

Masato, Mamako, and Shiraaase turned to look.

Beyond the violent family squabble, beyond the menacing family tea party, and beyond the lovely family knitting time were...three girls staring through the window.

Amante pointed directly at Masato, and then jerked her finger back. A clear "Get out here."

"......Uh...me?"

He'd been summoned.

His party was glued to the inside of the glass, watching him intently. Part of him wondered why they didn't just come with him, but they were clearly staying inside no matter what he said.

Outside the Mom Shop, Masato faced the Heavenly Kings alone.

"'Sup. You're all doing well, then?"

"Yeah, thanks. We stole your fight and all, but without our skills, we couldn't do anything, and we only survived because Hahako showed up to rescue us, but I'm not explaining about *that*."

"Wow, really?"

"Saaaad, but truuuue. Amante wound up clutched tight in Hahako's aaaarms, sleeping like a baaaby. I couldn't belieeeeve it."

"Seeing her sleeping so peaceful-like, I nearly busted a gut."

"Shut up, both of you! Just drop it already! That's not what we're here for!"

Amante grabbed a fistful of Masato's shirt, glaring at him from so close, their noses almost touched.

"Listen here, Masato Oosuki—it's your fault the Libere Rebellion was destroyed."

"Isn't that a good thing? You should be grateful."

"Don't be ridiculous! We don't give a damn about the Master—after all, she was actually a mother the whole time! But now we've got nowhere to go! No money, nothing!"

"Perfect! Forget the whole Rebellion thing! Start new lives! ...Look, there's someone positively itching to look after you."

Hahako was behind the three girls, watching them from the shadow of a building.

Amante seemed well aware of this but didn't look. Instead, she fixed Masato with an even fiercer glare.

"Well, we accidentally owe her now. But that doesn't mean we're accepting all she offers! Our ideals remain unwavering. That's why…"

"Why what?"

"As those who struggle against maternal tyranny, we challenge you to a final battle!"

Amante, Sorella, Fratello—three sets of eyes, gleaming with determination. All boring into Masato.

Afterword

Thank you. This is Inaka.

Volume eight has arrived—an auspicious number, symbolizing prosperity to come! I owe this to all of you. You have my gratitude.

This volume has a mom team-up! And *her* mother finally appears, making for a grand-scale family tale I hope you all enjoyed.

Once again I owe a tremendous debt to Iida Pochi.; my editor, K; and everyone in editing, publishing, and sales. This release is the result of all their contributions.

Meicha is working on the *Do You Love Your Mom* manga, and the second volume has been released, so I'd like to celebrate that as well as express my gratitude.

And to all the staff helping with the *Do You Love Your Mom* anime: I can't wait for the broadcast to begin in July 2019. I know you're all hard at work, and I wish you the best.

I'd also like to say a word to the readers who have written to me.

Thank you! I never imagined anyone would be writing to me personally!

I have received detailed opinions of my work, as well as suggestions and requests. I can't possibly make all of these come true, but they do help. I'll do what I can, and I hope you'll continue to follow me in my work.

And finally.

To my nephew, who, like Masato, is now in his first year of high school:

Go on and make an absolute fool of yourself. And then tell me all about it so I can sneak it into my own writing.

From your writer uncle, who spares no family member.

Early spring 2019, Dachima Inaka

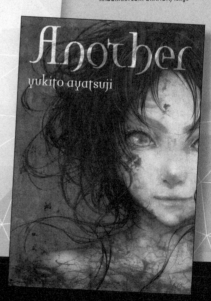